A DESIRABLE PROPERTY

by

NICOLE DERE

CHIMERA

A Desirable Property first published in 2002 by
Chimera Publishing Ltd
PO Box 152
Waterlooville
Hants
PO8 9FS

Printed and bound in Great Britain by
Omnia Books Ltd, Glasgow.

The characters and situations in this book are entirely imaginary and bear no relation to any real person or actual happening.

A DESIRABLE PROPERTY

Nicole Dere

This novel is fiction – in real life practice safe sex

'Turn,' she went on. 'This way. Bend over the wheel again. Put your arms up and hold on.'

She made me turn around and spread myself with my front resting against the huge tyre. Obediently I stretched my arms up on either side of its thickness and grasped the oily metal supports. My breasts were squashed against the rubber now, as were my tummy and the insides of my spread-eagled thighs. She did not fasten my wrists but just left me clinging there, and a second later I understood why; she needed to use the leather belt as an instrument of chastisement. With the buckle end firmly wrapped around her fist, she brought it down in a flaring line of fire across the centre of my exposed buttocks. I screamed and twisted free of the wheel, clutching at my stinging flesh.

Part One – Jane's Story

Chapter One

I woke up just as the cabin lights came on for the end of the in-flight movie. Carl was still sleeping. His brow furrowed in a frown of irritation, his thin face stirred slightly on the hard little pillow, and then he sank back into full sleep once more. I studied his still youthful looking features with an almost shocking sense of voyeurism. It wasn't often I got the chance to catch him so off guard. Relaxed, his face still showed that grace and handsomeness that slipped over at times into a beauty that might almost be considered femininely soft.

Beautiful youth. That was still the phrase that sprang automatically to mind when I recalled the first time I had seen him. I loved looking back on those early meetings when we had been so infatuated with each other. They were the golden times, the best of times, as they say. So much had changed in the four years that came after. Even two years ago, when we bowed to custom and agreed to mark our partnership by marriage, I was beginning to have those secret doubts, scarcely expressed even to myself, that our relationship would continue to blaze on magnificently, happily-ever-after. But wasn't that the way with all lovers and relationships the world over? Nothing that precious, that intense, could last forever. It is part of the human condition that everyone changes and adapts. Perhaps this fresh start, this new African setting – we were nearly there, the plane would be landing in an hour or so – would be the answer to our amorous status quo.

Something must be done, I told myself, painfully caught in a very uncomfortable introspective moment hanging between heaven and earth. Things could still be resolved, could still possibly be saved, between us. I felt hot, actually flushed with emotions, and I squirmed with shame in my seat as I vividly recalled yesterday afternoon in the anonymous luxury of the airport hotel in London…

The tension crackled and hovered between us like electricity. It was the first time we had really been alone together, with time to spare, for days, after the round of parties, farewells and meetings to prepare for Carl's prestigious posting to his firm's East African office.

'You lucky bastards!' I knew that was how everybody saw us. The good-looking young couple, everything going for us, winging off to an exciting new life together. And it was true – or could be true, if only we could somehow tear ourselves free of all the shadows that trailed like cobwebs after us in our personal relationship.

Sex. That is why I was blushing now, because the word kept hammering brutally in my brain, even as I automatically refuted it with scathing contempt. Love, say love, that's what it is, not just the animal rutting you're conjuring. But the mocking voice of my own libido went on lashing me with its scorn until I felt tears pricking behind my eyes in the capsuled privacy. I saw again, and felt, Carl's eyes on me as I undressed, ashamed and yet making it something of a peep show as I slipped off my skirt and my top, moving round in my sexy new underwear, knowing I looked good and letting him catch a leisurely eyeful. Bending my arms up behind me to unhook the mesh of the bra, aware that my nipples already showed mistily through it, their tiny points nearly thrusting out of the gossamer material, tingling with rubbery hardness and a desire to be caressed. Thumbs hooked at my hips I eased down my tiny briefs and sat on the edge of the wide bed to slide them in a tangle off my feet.

Without looking at him, I could feel his eyes burning into me. My heart thundered, and between my thighs my sex throbbed with fierce urgency. How many weeks was it since we had made love? The length of time could almost be measured in months rather than weeks. Certainly we had not made love the previous night in the luxurious bed, its cool wide loneliness seeming like acres when I curled to sleep, with Carl still drinking with his buddies down at the bar.

'If you loved me, you'd want to fuck me!' How many times I had longed to scream that at him. But of course I was too well bred, too civilised – we both were – to hurl such crude truths at each other. Besides, I was constantly telling myself that wasn't true anyway. Even if we didn't fuck, the love was still there, somewhere. Somehow. The heat of shame burnt fiercer at the torment of memory.

My unfaithfulness – such an old-fashioned word, my smart brain sneered, even though the word carried all the weight of its undiminished condemnation for me. Less than two weeks ago I had lain in another bed, with my legs bent up around Peter's sweating waist, my nails digging into his humping shoulders while his prick skewered me in an agony and ecstasy which drove me at last to a mindless coming, ankles crossed, pink heels hammering on his pounding buttocks. 'Oh God, I needed that!' I sobbed, and shrivelled with shame afterwards at the naked, desperate truth of my cry.

Carl is unfaithful too, I reminded myself, trying to ease my tender conscience, just as I had through all the clandestine fucks of my affair with Peter. I had no real proof though, not one shred of evidence. I couldn't convince myself, no matter how hard I tried, that he actually was unfaithful to me. Instead, I believed that Carl had gone off sex, gone off me. It didn't really help to make me feel any better. Nor did the even greater subterfuge of trying to tell myself that I loved Peter bolster my self-esteem any. I was in love with Peter's kisses, with Peter's hands, with his all too rampant cock, with our burning physical hunger. It was better than all the frustrated, lonely playing with myself I had been doing for so long. I was tired of the teasing masturbation that went on behind the locked bathroom door, under the fragrant lather of my bath. Being with Peter was no worse than that, anyway, I unsuccessfully argued with myself over and over again.

Then yesterday, as I sat perched on the end of the bed in the hotel room, like some naked tart, I suddenly felt that Carl and I might make our first move towards this long awaited fresh start. My heart, and my cunt, were throbbing with the need and want for it. I lifted my eyes nervously, shyly, caught his burning look, and the wordless communication leapt like sparks across the gulf of our estrangement. He lunged at me, knocking me backwards, his clothed body thrusting against me, his hands clawing, devouring, his open mouth possessing mine, tongue penetrating, moaning and shaking with passion. And, perversely, my hand caught his wrist as his palm fitted over the curve of my vulva, his fingers stroked at my dark pubis, prodded at the dampness of my labia. Why? I could wonder now, belatedly, bemused at my contrariness, my acute mistiming. 'No!' I gasped. 'Wait, let me have my bath first. Come and talk to me.'

And in my stupid mood of cock-tease I made him sit, watch me slide and slither, stand and wash myself, every intimate curve and plane of my flesh, while he stared avidly, eyes bright, scarcely talking while I prattled on lightly, wickedly, of the new life ahead of us, our great African adventure, as though the last thing on my mind was my screaming desire to be screwed to exhaustion.

Back in the bedroom, damply fragrant with perfume and talc, my dark little snatch fluffed up, my sweet sex dewy with anticipation, I let the towel fall, spread myself on my back on the bed, lewdly, in a come-and-fuck-me pose, my right leg drawn up and bent at the knee, thighs parted, presenting my sex to him like a bitch in heat. Which was exactly how I felt. 'Get your clothes off,' I growled, and he hastened to obey.

The nightmare developed slowly; unlike his tumbling haste as he tore off his gear and fell on me with that animal fury. His kisses, his hands, his fingers dug like claws into the yielding softness of my breasts and of my pliant bottom, spreading my thighs. 'Take it easy,' I panted, only half pretending to be afraid, excited by his lust yet perversely still wanting to slow it down, to tease it out to the exquisite limit. And then I felt his prick, wet and slimy, smearing my belly and the insides of my thighs as he lunged at me, again and again, buckling, softly impotent and incapable of penetrating me. His cry was of utter despair.

'No, no,' I gasped, holding him on top of me by force, feeling the stiffening of his muscles, everywhere except in those vital few inches of penis trapped between our heaving loins. 'It's all right. Wait, just take it easy. It'll be all right.' And I meant it. My own throbbing hunger was temporarily calmed by my compassion, by my wish to help him. I remembered how clumsy our first attempts at lovemaking had been, and how it had been up to me to get it right, to get him safely inside me, to take charge. I had loved it, it had felt great at the time, and when our flesh fused it was even more wonderful just to let go, to surrender to the power that shot through every fibre of my being, and to know we were both equally helpless in its thrall.

If I didn't come when he did he would wait until we had both recovered a little, and then slowly rekindle the passion, playing with me, with my breasts, suckling them. Then he would let his tongue and lips and teeth trail all over me, from my face and my neck down to my breasts, belly, thighs, legs, feet, and all the way down to my toes. Then, inch by slow inch, he would move up again until I was once more a mass of screaming need, before his mouth and his delicate fingers honed in on the wet and beating centre of my want, his tongue curling, lapping up the cleft of my vulva to the tiny nub of sensation, his fingers now deep and working rhythmically inside me. My buttocks clenched and my belly rose, buffeting him as I howled in the lost apocalypse of my coming.

I felt so ashamed afterwards that the tears always came. I lay there, eyes shut, returning slowly while his soaked face lay across my thigh. I couldn't look at him until I had been to the bathroom, cleaned myself and composed myself to face his love again. I was always aware in that first gentle, post-sex kiss, of where those lips and tender tongue had been only moments before.

Now, in the hotel, I had to go on playing the whore, the temptress, and I rolled him off me, lay across his stiff body, sensing the depth of his shame, his wish now only to flee the scene. I held him, by will as much as by strength, captured that flaccid prick, shrunk and shrouded in its collar of foreskin, slimy with his copious emission. It was so slippery and diminutive I could only hold on to it with difficulty, gently caressing it with my fingers. Then I bent, felt my hair stroking his belly, and then mingle with the black curls of his pubes, and let my lips pucker and kiss the folds of his penis, my tongue lapping at its brown satin softness. My thumb and finger slipped back the hood of his foreskin, bared the shiny tip of the helm with its narrow little slit. My tongue flickered, tasted the salty tang of juice, then I pushed my fingers down harder and felt the responsive convulsion, the swelling, and I closed my parted lips over it, took the entire head in my mouth and sucked deeply, slowly, until it swelled more, filling the warm wet cave of my mouth to its roof.

His prick beat so strongly, I thought with a feeling of mingled disappointment and delight that he was about to come in my mouth. My neck muscles tensed. In spite of myself I jerked instinctively and his prick emerged, with an audible little plop. Contritely, I captured it, smothered it into me again. The helm was clear now, and I could feel the flange where it rose from the thickening shaft. I let it free of my mouth once more and began to lap at it greedily with long strokes of my tongue, up from near the base of his balls to the swollen ridge of his helm, my fingers continuing to massage its warm, throbbing length, pressing it into his belly, nestling its head among the nest of his pubic hair. I would have got him stiff, would have climbed on him, fitted him into my vagina, rode him to a proper coupling, I was sure, when suddenly with a mighty heave which took me by surprise, he dislodged me. He gave a growl of pure pain and rage and flung me sprawling, then rolled over onto me, reversing our positions. He struck me an almighty slap across the outside of my thigh with his open palm; a ringing blow that sent fire darting through me and brought up a fiery red print on my skin still visible twenty-four hours later.

Yelping with startled anguish I found myself stretched on my back, my legs apart. His fingers were hooked in my thighs as he spread them wide, exposing my cleft mercilessly. Then his hot face was thrust at me, at my sex, rooting, gnawing, lapping, in a bestial frenzy that stunned me – until I felt my wayward flesh responding to this brutality with an urgency too powerful to resist. My hands fell from his hunched shoulders, my head fell back on the tangled coverlet, and I groaned, my belly lifted now in helpless cooperation at his rutting, buried face. The feeling of want and hunger and excitement spread remorselessly, until that moment when I lost sense of everything, except that pounding rush of sensation carrying me up and up to the explosive force of an orgasm that ripped through me, and left me spent and sobbing helplessly in its consuming wake.

Now, in the newly lit cabin of the plane, his eyes opened, looked into mine from a few inches away, and darted guiltily aside as if he, too, at that instant, was sharing the awful memory of those minutes after the cunnilingus on the hotel bed, when my sobbing had quietened and he pushed up from between my spread thighs and hurried without a word to the bathroom. The water ran, splashed noisily, and he emerged again, clad in a robe, which he kept on while he hastily pulled on his briefs and then completed dressing, picking up his scattered clothing without glancing at my sprawled nakedness.

'I'm going back down to the bar,' he said. 'I'll give Jerry a ring. See you later.' His voice was guttural and harsh with enmity. I lay still after he had gone, too weary and apathetic to move. When I did finally move, my face felt scalded with shame at seeing the dark wet patch on the cover where my parted thighs had been.

My gloomy reflections quashed the brief glimmering of hope for our future. We sat in silence as the stewards brought round breakfast, and then hastily cleared the trays and made brisk preparation for our landing. The disembodied voice from the flight deck began to speak, and then abruptly lapsed into silence again. Nothing happened. The new redness of a tropical sun slanted into the cabin, tingeing everything with its strange old, gold light. Seats were brought upright, and we waited to hear the imminent landing being announced.

There was a sudden stirring, a an odd sense of confusion, and two of the flight crew girls came hurrying along the aisle from the forward end of the aircraft. I glanced up curiously at their faces. My heart faltered, and a great lurch of terror speared me. Their expressions were almost identical – sheer horror. Behind them were two men and a girl. I saw only her short blonde hair and attractive face. Then all three were shouting and brandishing what my incredulous gaze registered as stocky automatic weapons. There were some gasps and one or two muted cries went up from the seats around us. One of the stewards stumbled, went down on one knee, and the man immediately behind her gave her a hefty kick that sent her sprawling full length at our feet.

'This is a hijack! You are all prisoner! Do not move or you die!' The man screamed, his voice penetratingly shrill. He reached down, grabbed the weeping steward by her dark hair and dragged her to her feet. He flung her stumbling forward again, thrusting her down towards the rear of the plane.

His companion moved too. The blonde girl, dressed in military style khaki shirt and slacks, stayed in the front compartment, in the doorway that led to the flight cabin. 'Sit still!' she yelled. 'You are now all hostages!' Her English, and her control, were superior to those of her fellow terrorists, and they made her presence, as well as her gestures with the gun, all the more menacing. 'We have radioed our demands. We will land shortly. Do not move or speak, or I will shoot, okay?'

Chapter Two

'Please, can I go to the toilet?' My voice came out as a scratchy whisper. The blonde girl, who was coming round collecting our passports, studying each photo carefully then scrutinising the features of its owner, stared at me, her grey eyes cool, expressionless. I felt my face burning. 'I've wet myself,' I murmured pathetically. It was true. I hadn't realised I had done so until I was shocked to feel the small circle of damp at my bottom, the unpleasant clinging of the triangle of silk to my crotch. We were still caught in the stunning unreality of what was happening to us. I had no idea how long we had all been sitting there transfixed while the three terrorists moved rapidly up and down the central aisle of the plane. And there was another, a fourth hijacker, in the flight cabin.

The girl's eyes stared coldly at me, and I lowered my gaze. 'Jane Freeman?' She was reading my details. 'You are British?' I nodded. She glanced across at Carl. 'You are her husband?' An incongruously innocent smile spread across her face. 'Your wife is not very brave, I think, to piss herself, yes?' Her foreign accent was slight but noticeable, and she was undeniably attractive. She hesitated, and then said, 'Okay, come, but do not try to be brave.' She laughed. 'I think not, but if you try anything, I will shoot.'

I moved, getting awkwardly to my feet, suddenly deeply

embarrassed at the feel of my crumpled skirt, wondering if it was stained. There was a faint patch in the dip of the seat. 'What are you doing?' The sharpness of her words made me jump. I had been bending to pick up my small cabin bag, stuffed beneath my chair.

'My… my toilet bag… my things,' I stammered. 'I have a change—'

'No! Come!' She cradled her gun in her right arm and the fingers of her left hand dug in hard on the softness of my upper arm as she pulled me out into the aisle. She turned to one of her companions. He had swarthy features, handsome in an aquiline way. A thick drooping black moustache, neatly trimmed, marked his lower face. 'I take this one to the toilet,' she said. 'She has pissed herself with fear.' He grinned and moved aside to let us pass. My breath rasped in a sob, and I kept my head down, feeling the need to cry welling up inside me.

When she shut the door of the tiny compartment on us, there was scarcely room for us to stand without touching. She laid her weapon down on the shelf beside the small hand basin. The light seemed to bounce from the shiny walls all round me; its brilliance hurt my eyes. 'Come!' she snapped curtly. 'Take off your panties. Clean yourself.'

I had wanted my bag because, as well as my toilet things, it contained a spare pair of knickers. I paused helplessly for a second until, with a hiss of impatience, she plunged her hands under the thin material of my skirt. I felt her fingernails scratch my skin as she sought the elastic of my briefs, and then hauled them down my hips and thighs. With a whimper of fright I took over from her, bending awkwardly and shuffling them clear of my feet. I had to slip off my sandals in order to do so.

She seized the back of my skirt and lifted it until my bottom was bared. 'This will soon dry,' she said. 'Unless you want to remove it too.'

'No,' I gasped, horrified at the notion of being made to walk back through the plane naked from the waist down.

'Here.' Her tone was still one of irritation. She was thrusting a box of wet-wipes at me, from the shelf over the basin. I began to cry softly, I couldn't help it, overcome with shame and terror while I hastily wiped between my legs, my pubis, and the cleft of my bottom. I was deeply aware of her steady gaze on me. She grabbed my light skirt again, holding it up above my belly. 'What is this?' she asked.

The change of tone startled me. She was smiling again, nodding amusedly at the red smudge on the side of my right thigh, where Carl had slapped me the day before. 'I... I must have knocked myself,' I stammered unconvincingly.

She chuckled, and I flinched as her cool fingers passed lightly across it. 'It looks more like a handprint. A smack, you say. Your husband did this to you?'

'No, no, I – oh!' I tried to deny it, but she spun me round and aimed a swift swat at my bare bottom. I felt its sharp sting. Instinctively my hand flew down to touch, and touched her own before I jerked it away again.

'You like – when you love?' She nodded down at my bared flesh, and my face flushed again. Tears sprang up into my eyes. I shook my head and she laughed, a low, rippling kind of sound. 'You have a very nice ass, yes? Made for spanking.'

There was an excruciating pause while I stared down, my gaze misted with tears. My skirt was still caught up and I could see the dark bush of my pubes standing out against the pale of my belly and thighs. 'Please,' I whispered feebly, the tears starting to spill down my cheeks.

Abruptly she pushed me, and I sat down on the low lavatory pedestal. I could feel the rub of her slacks on my knees as she stood over me. Her hands pressed firmly on my shoulders. 'You'd better do another pee. I don't want another accident.'

I shook my head, and then yelped as she grabbed my hair with one hand and slapped me stingingly across the cheek with her other. 'Do as you're told, *bitch*,' she hissed.

I cried quietly, snuffling abjectly. I pushed out my belly, squeezing my bladder, and managed to produce a brief dribble of urine. 'That's better.' She was smiling, her voice calm, almost pleasant again. 'You just have to obey, that's all. Then everything is okay.' She was running her hand through my hair now, smoothing it. Her palm cupped round my neck, and then my still smarting jaw. 'Get up.'

There was hardly room for me to do so because she was standing so close. As I rose my skirt was still caught between us. Her body was touching mine now and I tensed, trembling with renewed fear. Her hand moved round the back of my neck, then slid down to my hollowed back, pulling me into her embrace. 'I like good girls,' she smiled, her eyes holding me with an intensely smouldering look. I gazed back like a paralysed rabbit, unable to look away. Her lips were within inches of mine; I could feel her sweet, warm breath.

'Do you like girls?' Her voice was thick, shocking in its intimacy. I saw her honey-coloured throat working, knew she was about to kiss me. I flinched and moved my mouth away from hers, then felt her hand dig cruelly into the back of my head, fingers talon-like in my hair, holding my face towards her. Her lips closed over mine in a raw kiss. I felt the hardness of her teeth, her probing tongue, and with a sob, I opened my mouth, yielding it to her. Her tongue plunged in, possessing, draining me of strength, and I sagged against her, felt her pliant body pressed hard against me, her arms holding my limp frame to her vibrant one. My head spun, I couldn't breathe. I hung giddily, gulping for air when her lips finally released mine.

Her hands moved under my skirt with firm tenderness, tracing my thighs, my hips, and then cradling the tautened rounds of my bottom, savouring their contours. The crisp roughness of her khaki clothing pressed against me. She kissed me again, gently, lingeringly, and I kept my mouth to hers submissively open. I shivered at the blatantly amorous strokes of her hands about my bare flanks. Her short fingernails scratched lightly as she traced the deep groove of my buttocks.

Her small breasts lifted the material of her shirt, and she sounded breathless as she gave a little laugh and released me. 'I think I could teach you to love girls,' she teased. 'But we'd better go, bitch, or they'll think we're having fun in here, yes?'

I kept my eyes down, staring at my feet as we made our way back to my seat, imagining all the frightened stares on me. I was deeply conscious of my nudity under my thin skirt. 'Don't catch cold,' my captor chuckled when at last I reached the empty chair beside Carl. I could still feel the faint dampness underneath me as I sat.

'You all right?' Carl asked. His voice sounded shocking, and I gasped with fright.

'I said no talking,' the blonde girl said, with quiet menace. My terrified eyes fixed pleadingly on Carl. Somehow I knew what his tortured thoughts were, knew how he still felt diminished in front of me, that the knowledge of his failure to fuck me still lay between us.

'Look,' he said tensely, 'my wife's very frightened. We all are. What are you going to do with us? Why aren't we landing?'

'Please,' the girl said reasonably. She leaned forward, over me, motioned for Carl to come closer, and he too leaned forward until his head was close to hers. Her right hand moved with blurring speed, formed into a fist that smashed hard into Carl's mouth. He shot back, his eyes wide with incredulous shock and pain. A thin line of blood trickled down from the split in his lower lip and his fingers went up to the wound, stanched the red drops, smearing them on his chin.

'Your wife has more sense than you have,' the girl said coolly. Her two associates had stepped forward, raising their guns. Now they relaxed, grinning broadly. Carl leaned back against the pillow, his face drained of colour, his dark eyes brooding. His hand was still up to his swollen lip.

I gazed up at her pleadingly. 'Don't hurt us,' I whispered. She hung over me, and again caressed the back of my neck briefly.

'Just be good,' she smiled. 'And don't get alarmed.

Remember, you have no more knickers, yes?'

It wasn't until much later that we learnt the delay in giving us permission to land at Leontondo was all part of a subterfuge, to hide from the world the prearranged connivance between President Koloba and the hijackers. While we circled above the Great Lake, for what seemed endless hours, the girl, whom I accurately deduced was German, spoke over the tannoy to us, standing with the gun cradled loosely in her arm. 'There are several bombs onboard.' She lifted what looked like a remote control panel that was clipped onto the military belt at her waist. 'My comrades and I each have one of these. A single push on the button and – pouf! Up we go, all of us together!' Again that incongruous, wide smile, so beautifully clean cut. 'So, even if you take one of us out, there are the other three. Any one of us can end it all instantly. But I know you won't be foolish. You wish to live, yes?' There were some low, heartfelt murmurs of assent.

Although no one spoke, obeying the original orders for silence, there were sounds, each one of which terrified me anew. An elderly woman fainted, and her decrepit husband started sobbing, crying out for help. They moved her to the rear and let him and another woman, who claimed to be a nurse, tend to her. Then there were a number of families with infants and older children. Quickly seating was rearranged, these families being herded in the rearmost seats while I sat and trembled and prayed that no one would try anything foolish and start the bullets flying, or worse.

'We are going to land at Leontondo,' the German girl

announced. 'We are almost out of fuel. Fasten your belts. And move slowly.' Her grey eyes caught my frightened stare among the rows of pale faces, and again I received that dazzling smile. 'Do not be afraid, Jane. You are still dry, yes?'

We came down with sickening speed through the thinning grey wisps of cloud, and then there were several shrieks and gasps as the great sheet of water appeared below us, so terrifyingly close. We skimmed along, seemingly only feet above its rippling surface, and then, with that characteristic muffled squeal and a discernible bump, the wheels touched onto the runway, the engines roared in reverse thrust, and soon we were slowing, turning, and taxiing to our appointed station far from any of the low terminal buildings or other planes.

At last we were still, and I let out my breath in a wavering sigh of relief.

With a sense of shock, I stared down at my hands clasped in Carl's sweating grip, and wondered how long we had been holding on to each other. I looked at him, tried to smile, and knew how pathetic my effort must look. I could see the vivid ripe redness of his swollen lip, the tiny flakes of dried blood remnants on his chin. He smiled back tightly, but my stomach lurched as I recognised in his brown eyes the cold clutch of fear that mirrored my own.

Chapter Three

There was an eerie silence when the plane's engines switched off, and then all the other machinery, including the air conditioning. Through the thick glass of the porthole next to Carl I could see only a few yards of cracked tarmac, and then long swathes of dead-looking yellow grass which merged with the tawny, indistinct shimmer of the distant bush, liberally dotted with dark clumps of thorn trees. Suddenly I felt even more tense now that we were safely down, back on earth, the relief at landing safely swiftly dribbling away.

The girl took up her position by the door to the flight deck once more, and spoke into a hand mike. 'Now we wait. For humanitarian reasons, President Koloba permitted us to land here. The Leontondese government is passing on our demands, but we have decided that at this moment you have no right to know what you might be called upon to die for. Perhaps you will in good time.'

The wave of icy terror engulfed me. I stifled the scream that rose in my throat and my sweating hand clung to Carl's. I could scarcely take in her words for the sickening fear that possessed me. What the hell has all this to do with us, my reeling brain screamed in protest, you blonde German bitch? But of course I uttered no sound, just sat there, sweating and trembling.

She and one of her associates disappeared into the flight

cabin, leaving only one terrorist on guard, the shortest of them, a thickset, almost plump individual with thick stubble covering his chin and a heavily drooping moustache. His dark eyes blazed out over the rows of frightened countenances. The fretful whimpers and the cries of the youngsters from the back seemed appallingly loud. For fuck's sake, my mind protested frantically, why doesn't somebody shut those kids up? This guy looks as though he's just waiting for any excuse to open up with that gun of his.

Within an hour the interior of the plane was like an oven. I could feel my light cotton top clinging wetly to me, and the backs of my thighs on the upholstery felt as though I'd wet myself all over again. Beads of perspiration ran down my neck and trickled between my breasts, collecting in the folds of my naked thighs and tummy. The German girl came back, her tanned complexion shining with the heat, her short blonde hair clinging limply to her brow like a cap.

'We open the front door,' she said, and the waft of air that came blowing in was like the draught from an oven, but it was welcome nevertheless.

Then a tall, athletic-looking girl a few rows in front put her hand up like a child in school. Her hair was white-blonde and cut so short it was like spiky fuzz on top of her head. 'I have to go to the washroom.' The American drawl was very pronounced.

When she stood I could appreciate even more the statuesque beauty of her frame. She must have been about five-ten, her shoulders square, the muscles defined on her deep golden arms. She was wearing a skimpy sleeveless tank-top of olive green, which gave her a military appearance. It left a lot of her shoulders and her neck bare, but where it clung between the shoulder blades, there was a wide dark patch of sweat. As she turned to ease herself out into the aisle, I saw the contours of one full breast, the pointed nipple and its surround showing plainly in darkened outline against the material. Her legs were long, and her bottom looked gorgeous in the jeans, faded almost to white, which hugged her form.

The German gestured with her automatic. 'Come slowly.' She stepped warily in front of her. 'You are American slut, yes?'

'American yes – slut no,' the girl answered defiantly. She edged past the slim hijacker. Even though she was wearing only a pair of rubber thong sandals, she was at least half a head taller than the German.

'Your name, slut?'

The pretty young face flushed under its coating of sweat. 'Nicky Gimburg. And I told you – I'm no slut.'

As the tall figure squeezed past her, the German lifted her booted foot and thrust it hard into the behind of the American, propelling her forward a yard or so, almost making her fall. The American swung round with an expression of outrage. 'Hey! Cut that out!'

The girl in the khaki uniform moved menacingly, raising the automatic, and suddenly one of the stewardesses, a coloured girl whose beauty reflected her mixed parentage, came forward and reached out to take hold of the American girl. 'Take it easy, honey,' she muttered softly while the American stood there, bristling. I held my breath, as did many others, I'm sure.

'I think you'd better go and take your piss,' the German said after a nightmare pause. Her voice was calm again, with mocking superiority. 'Like all your countrymen, you seem to be full of it.'

She stood in the doorway of the toilet, holding it open with one foot, while Nicky Gimburg relieved herself, then, when the glowering figure had regained her seat, the German stood over her and pointed the stubby barrel of the weapon at her. 'Take off your top, slut!' There was a gasp, and then a hoarse screech of denial. Suddenly, the muzzle of the gun was thrust viciously at the girl's throat. She yelped in pain. 'Do you want me to blow your fucking head all over these nice people?' the hijacker yelled, and there was an assortment of screams and pleas.

'Do what she says!' a hysterical voice shrieked.

'Ahmed, if she moves, shoot her,' the German said, smiling wickedly, and behind her the taller of the two male hijackers we had seen nodded enthusiastically.

'Of course, Krista.' He grinned, eyes bulging in anticipation. Krista. Even in my terror my mind registered the name, glad to have something to call her at last.

She removed her gun from Nicky's throat. It left a vivid red mark on the golden skin. Deliberately, she laid it against the arm of the seat, reached down and very slowly pulled the top up, rolling it up her stomach, forcing it up until Nicky's folded arms prevented her from baring her breasts. 'You want to die, slut?' Krista breathed, her lips close to Nicky's ear.

All at once the American gave a convulsive sob and let her arms unfold to fall limply by her sides. Krista tugged the garment up, rolled it over her splendid breasts, which, braless, fell magnificently into view. Their rounds were paler than the surrounding tan. The centres were crowned with generous areolae, and the nipples themselves were large, raised prominently from the curves they centred. Now the little garment slid easily up and over the sleek blonde head.

'My, my,' Krista chuckled. The American's head was down, and those divine breasts were shaking with her desolate sobs. She kept her hands down at her sides, making no attempt to hide herself. 'You have nothing to be shy about. You have tits that would feed an army. Eh, Ahmed?'

'Very nice,' he chortled, feasting his eyes.

When Krista at last moved away Nicky's golden arms folded over her breasts. The cropped white head bent, and she cried softly to herself. I stared at her slender fingers, spread over her arms. They looked elegant, the clean nails unpainted, cut short and beautifully shaped.

It felt as if we were suspended in time trapped in that sweltering tube of metal. Soon the place stank from our combined sweat. Our captors seemed to suffer as much as we did. Even Krista's smart crispness wilted. The perspiration glistened on her face while her blonde hair darkened and hung in limp strands. Dark patches showed up on her khaki drill shirt, spreading out from the armpits. Before long the unpleasant atmosphere was made worse by the fetid stench that rose from the toilets and spread throughout the cabin.

Then everyone seemed to feel the urge to relieve themselves and the terrorists organised toilet trips, several rows at a time. It wasn't only bladders that were voided.

The flush system ceased to work, and the small compartments were soon overflowing. The air was rife with the pungent odour of shit. And then thirst became a major problem. The now bedraggled stewards, their blue jackets cast aside and their clinging white blouses showing every detail of the bras they wore beneath them, padded up and down the aisle constantly serving drinks. I glanced down as the coloured girl handed me a tiny can of something. I saw her bare feet, innocent of shoes and of the tights that were part of her uniform. Her dainty toenails were painted a deep magenta. For her lover? How long would it be before those pretty feet were opening for her partner?

Like many others, I actually managed to doze off for short intervals, hating each heart jarring return to consciousness and the nightmare of reality. No matter how hard I tried I could not keep myself from glancing at my watch, noting the hours creeping by with agonising slowness. Still no one talked, though there was a constant background of crying infants and the frantic efforts of parents to hush them, and also the pathetic whimpers of those lost in uneasy slumber.

At the first sign of action, there was heart-stopping panic again. The fourth hijacker, who had been closeted with the pilot and flight crew, appeared. I had assumed that Krista was the leader of the group, but it quickly became apparent that he was in charge, though his attitude towards the German girl was far less authoritative than to the two other male members of the team. He was very lean and actually very handsome. He was clean-shaven, and his olive complexion and close-cropped black hair gave him a Mediterranean look, although apart from the blonde German, we had no idea where they were from or what they wanted. It was not until later that we found out he was known as Khotan.

He had his arms full of passports, and he and Krista started to call out names, ordering these people to collect their hand baggage and to move out into the aisle. The sound of fresh weeping and furtive whispers rose on all sides. 'Do not worry!' he called strongly. 'We are setting you free. You see, we are not inhuman. Tell the authorities that.'

It became clear that the mothers and children, and the elderly of both sexes, were those who were departing first. There were touching scenes between the married couples who were being split up, tears, frantic kisses, several sobbing pleas from the wives that their husbands be allowed to go with them, but the leader shook his head. 'They will be safe,' he said. 'You will see them later. As long as everyone is not stupid, that is.'

Two hours later, there was another cull. More names were read out, a good number of them males. Ironically, there was a more relaxed air about both captors and captured now. We were allowed to talk, even to move around if we asked permission. I sank gratefully into Carl's embrace, and we both stretched out across the three seats. I savoured the feel of his arms tight around me, one touching the underside of my breasts. I was pressed against the backs of the seats and he fitted himself into me from behind. I pushed my bottom into his loins, very aware of my nakedness under my crumpled skirt, and felt the responsive bulge and throb of his penis under the restriction of his clothing as he slotted it into the cleft of my bottom.

At first, it was the comforting feel of his intimate embrace I sought, the security it brought me, but then, suddenly and shockingly, I felt my vaginal muscles spasming rhythmically and my buttocks clenching, thrusting back discreetly and stirring his beating prick to respond. I seized his wrist, pushed his hand down over my stomach, lower, letting him feel the tuft of my pubis under the flimsy material, and then guiding him between my thighs until I was holding his fingers over the damp, cushiony pad of my mons and he was touching the bare skin under the displaced hem of my skirt.

It grew dimmer as the short twilight faded, then outside the porthole was impenetrable blackness. The plane's electrical system was not working. The only light came from gas lamps placed near the front of the craft, so that we were all lying in deep shadow. It was this that made me bold, though part of me was still stunned by my sexual hunger in such weird and dangerous circumstances. I guided Carl's fingers more specifically until their tips pressed at the uppermost folds of my labia, and then into the slippery tissue that flowered open and streamed wetly at these caresses. I was grinding my bottom lewdly into him, clenching and unclenching, thrilling to the ever-fiercer beat of his engorged prick even through the layers of cloth that separated us. I offered my neck back, shuddering with pleasure when his teeth nibbled and he sucked at my flesh.

I gasped, turning my head towards his warm mouth. 'Jesus! I think – I think I'm going to come. Oh, don't stop, darling. Please duh – don't stop!'

I was gyrating madly now, thrusting forth my belly, pulling his hand ever tighter up into my vulva, gripping with my thighs, lost to everything except this pulsing, rising need...

'What you doing?' The words and the blinding glare of the torch beam shattered my private sex world like an explosion. I gasped, felt Carl pull away from me, and realised I was lying with my skirt up over my hips, baring my bottom and the dark shadow of my pubes. With a great sob of shame I squirmed round and up and tried to pull the dishevelled scrap of my skirt down over my naked flesh.

The dark shape of Krista stood over me, holding us in that merciless beam. She was grinning evilly. 'You cannot be British! I do not believe it. I thought you Brits did not like sex. Now I find you fucking even though you might be blown to the sky any minute!' She shook her head and her laugh mocked us. 'You hot bitch! Come with me, I cool you down.'

Carl was crouched awkwardly. He gave a kind of grunt and Krista casually swung the torch onto his scared features. 'Do not be brave, little man. And keep your cock in your trousers, yes? Otherwise I might blow it off.' She laughed again, and then jabbed my upper arm painfully with the barrel of the gun. 'Move!' Snivelling softly, I stumbled as I hastened to obey her.

She stopped and said something to the one known as Khotan, who was sitting just inside the open door of the flight cabin beside the radio equipment. I was waiting, standing next to one of the others, the thickset unshaven one, who was leering at me. Their leader, Khotan, gave a dismissive nod, and Krista pointed towards the gap of the open doorway, through which the warm night showed. There was a dim lamp at the head of a narrow flight of metal steps leading to the ground. It did not strike me until much later that the forward end of the aircraft was not lit up at all. Only the area of tarmac behind us, leading to the distant airport buildings, was brilliantly lit.

'Go on, down the steps,' Krista ordered. 'The night air might cool you a little, hot bitch.'

Once again came that sensation of all the strength draining from me. My legs shook and I gazed at her helplessly. She was going to shoot me. Down there in the tropical darkness, she was going to kill me. I sank in a heap on the top step. 'Please,' I sobbed brokenly. 'I'm sorry... I'll do anything. Please, I beg you.'

She kicked me on the thigh. 'Go on, bitch, I'm not going to hurt you. I told you, I'm just going to let you cool off a little.' She laughed, and I stumbled down the steps, weeping piteously. I could feel the hard metal on my bare feet.

'Please don't hurt me,' I blubbered, turning to her at the bottom of the steps. 'I'll do whatever you want – please!'

Even in the dimness of the light spilling down on us from above, I could see her look of contempt. With the gun she motioned me to move, and still burbling in terror, I obeyed. We stood in deep shadow now, right under the bulbous nose of the aircraft, which reared like a roof over us. The nose wheel, taller than me, was beside us.

'You really are a hot little bitch, aren't you, Jane?' she

said. 'Even now you want to fuck with your man, yes?'

'No, I – I just – we were cuddling – I wanted him to – to comfort me.' Desperately I fought to control my weeping, gulping in air.

She gave a harsh laugh. 'Is that what you call it? He had his hand up your cunt, bitch. He was fiddling with you.' I hung my head, weeping. Although my heart was still banging painfully in my ribs, I had the feeling that my cravenness, my display of helpless fear, might be my strongest ally. She was enjoying the spectacle of my degradation. That was what she wanted; I could tell she was excited by it. But her next words made me gasp with shock. 'Take your clothes off, bitch. What's left of them, at least.'

I gawped at her, my mouth open, and she pointed the gun at me, smiling. 'I won't tell you again…'

I unzipped the crumpled skirt and let it fall about my ankles, and then swiftly peeled the cotton top up over my head. I reached behind and unhooked my bra, and as my breasts were freed from the cups, I felt my perspiration drying coolly in the heavy warmth of the night air. The breeze played about my naked body as my hands came up to cross my arms over my breasts, but then one moved down to the dark little triangle of my pubis.

'Your tits are not large, baby,' she said, 'but they are cute. They are just as I like them…' I gasped again as she reached out and casually fondled me. My nipples were erect, and her thumb and forefinger pinched the right one with playful force, and then gave it a little tweak. 'Turn around,' she went on, her voice now little more than a whisper.

Trying still to stem my tears, I obeyed, and stiffened as I felt that same hand pass lingeringly over my bottom, stroking and tracing its contours. My buttocks clenched and dimpled as I reacted instinctively to the invasive touch. 'And a gorgeous little ass,' she breathed.

Even as I cried and trembled, I felt deep inside a sensation of profound relief, for I suddenly knew she would not harm me after all.

'Over here, baby.' Her voice was soft, crooning, heavy with sexuality, a lover's voice. My legs were like jelly but I had no thought other than to obey. To my surprise, she gestured for me to stand against the huge wheel with my back to it, and then she pushed me up against it. She had put the gun on the ground, but I had no intention of trying to resist her, or to try and get to it. I felt the strangely smooth rubber on my bottom, and then against my hollowed back and shoulder blades as she gently moulded me to its giant curve.

I was leaning back now, totally vulnerable to her, my breasts and tummy thrust forward, only my toes touching the tarmac. The rubber was still warm. I stared up into the blackness of the compartment where the wheel was housed when raised – an oily cavern of pipes and cables.

'Lift your arms, Jane.' Her murmured command came from beside my ear. I obeyed, and felt my breasts lift and tauten. She was using a belt to bind my wrists tightly together, and then she lashed them to an upright metal stanchion, one of the struts of the wheel. Thus I was secured, pinioned, my pale body curved back, and she took full advantage of my helplessness.

Despite my best efforts to restrain myself I began to

weep and shiver, first with shock, and then, incredibly, with excitement. Her hands were surprisingly tender as they passed all over my body, from my thighs up to my throat, squeezing, stroking and rousing. 'Have you ever loved with a girl?' she whispered, her breath hot on my cheek. 'Have you truly?'

'Nuh – never,' I sobbed, and then her lips sealed my mouth. Her tongue pressed, and with a convulsive shudder, I opened, and it drove possessively into me. I could scarcely breathe when, at last, our lips parted again only for hers to move down, pausing at my exposed throat, and then to alight on my uplifted breasts. Her tongue flickered, feather light, around a nipple, and I was afire with need. I cried out softly at the melting sensation that flowed right through me as her lips closed around my teat and suckled hungrily and deeply, her face pressed into the softness of my flesh. Then she moved across to my other breast and I whimpered, lost to the sensations coursing through every part of me.

That wicked tongue flickered in the shallow little recess of my navel, and I sucked in my belly as desire sparked like electricity through my flesh until I thought I would faint. 'No,' I wept instinctively when I felt her face against my mound, her nose and lips rooting in the damp curls of my pubic hair... and on down into that running, swollen tissue of my sex, burning now with its hunger, awash with my running excitement, pungent with the odour of sweat and juice and sexual urgency. Her tongue lapped at the very centre of my need, devouring that tangy, salty crevice, which lifted in helpless response as though returning her passionate kisses from that other, hot mouth.

I groaned, begging for release, murmuring over and over, 'Please... *please*...' I felt her arm slip under my left knee and she lifted my leg, holding it high to the side, opening my loins even more blatantly to her burrowing caresses, and I drove my mound into her, lost to everything but the rushing crisis. Two of her fingers slid easily into the pulsing orifice of my vagina, which spasmed madly, and I writhed and shook and sobbed at the storm of my coming, which totally consumed me, my pale body threshing like a victim on the rack, arched in the velvet darkness of the tropical night.

Chapter Four

I was hardly aware of where I was until I felt my pinioned arms being untied, and my body eased from the curve of the tyre. Pain and shame flooded over me in equal quantities, and I wept forlornly. I sagged in Krista's embrace, and she held me to her. I could feel her clothing rubbing against my skin and her lips nuzzling my tearstained face. Then her thumb and fingers dug into my chin and she held me while she clamped her mouth over mine in one more savagely passionate kiss. 'There,' she panted triumphantly, 'taste your own come, you sexy little bitch.'

I sobbed, but she did not let me go. Instead she shook my tragic face, her features thrust close to mine. 'It was good, was it not?' she hissed. 'Tell the truth, bitch.'

'Yuh – yes!' I howled, tears of shame scalding me. 'It was good!' I could not deny the sick truth that overwhelmed me.

'Jane, my lover, I cannot now let you go without I punish you. You understand? You are my captive.' I instantly forgot my shame and stared at her in fresh alarm. 'Turn,' she went on. 'This way. Bend over the wheel again. Put your arms up and hold on.'

She made me turn around and spread myself with my front resting against the huge tyre. Obediently I stretched my arms up on either side of its thickness and grasped the oily metal supports. My breasts were squashed against the rubber now, as were my tummy and the insides of my spread-eagled thighs. She did not fasten my wrists but just left me clinging there, and a second later I understood why; she needed to use the leather belt as an instrument of chastisement. With the buckle end firmly wrapped around her fist, she brought it down in a flaring line of fire across the centre of my exposed buttocks. I screamed and twisted free of the wheel, clutching at my stinging flesh.

'Lie back down!' she snarled, gesturing at the tyre, and in spite of the agony I obeyed her once more, clinging convulsively while I begged through my tears for mercy. *Splat!* The belt fell a second time, overlaying that first red stripe with another one, and my bottom clenched and jumped beneath the impact. I screamed, but somehow managed to keep myself bent to that obscene rubber, my sobs coming in harsh gasps. She struck quickly a third and a fourth time, and my bottom was on fire, it was all I could do not to let my hand claw at my throbbing skin. I could feel the raised welts over the quivering surface of my flesh.

'Oh, please no, no more!' Two more blows followed before the punishment ended and I was allowed to raise myself from the wheel. At every movement the pain in my beaten bottom was intense. My hands moved automatically to ease the stinging, but the lightest touch made me wince and whimper. The tips of my fingers brushed the tracery of angry raised bumps, which throbbed abominably. I stood in front of her, my head bent, my hands carefully stroking my bottom while my sobs died to a pitiful weeping.

To my amazement, she took me gently in her arms again, and this time her kisses were soft and tender, as were her hands as they held me close. 'I had to do that, darling Jane,' she crooned, her lips against my ear. 'I must be tough with you, you know that. But you are my girl now. Obey me and you will be fine.' She chuckled. 'And that randy husband of yours also. But remember, no more fucking, yes? Not while you are mine. Don't forget that, Jane.'

She found my scraps of clothing and helped me put on and fasten my skirt. 'I don't think you need this, yes? It can go with your knickers.' She dropped my bra carelessly to the ground, and I pulled my top over my head. I winced with pain as I climbed back aboard the plane. Each step sent a dart of throbbing agony through my poor bottom.

Even in the subdued light, I felt every pair of eyes was fixed on me and I could see the shame written on my features as I hobbled back to my seat. Then fresh horror gripped me when I saw that Carl was not there. I turned in panic. 'W-what's happened?' I blurted. 'Where's my husband?'

'One of the guards took him,' the American girl turned and told me, her face expressing her sympathy. I noticed she was wearing the olive tank-top once more.

Krista noticed, too. 'Why you cover your tits?' she demanded angrily.

Nicky Gimburg flushed and tried unsuccessfully to hide her nervousness, her full lips turned down in a touchingly childlike pout. She nodded towards the front of the plane. 'I asked and he said I could. The one by the radio.'

She meant Khotan, the leader of the group. Krista scowled ferociously at Nicky, and in return she strove to maintain an air of defiance. Krista leaned towards the seated figure, and Nicky could not help flinching away slightly. 'Take care, slut,' the German growled. 'I fix you good, yes?'

'Please,' I gasped desperately, reaching in my fear for Krista's arm. 'You promised – don't let them hurt Carl.'

Krista thrust me off, pushed me down into the seat, and I gasped again at the stab of pain in my tender rear as it made contact with the upholstery. She stomped off to the front of the plane and stood talking to one of the gang, the tallest of them. He smiled, and nodded towards the rear of the plane. Krista then came back down the aisle to me. I blushed, aware that many people were eyeing us curiously.

'Is okay,' she told me. 'Your man wanted to go to the lavatory. The ones at the back are not quite so disgusting as these up front.'

I squirmed around uncomfortably on the seat, trying to ease the throbbing in my bottom. I think the shock of the cruel and unjust punishment, and the huge relief of finding that I was not to be killed, had blunted my confusion about what had happened before the thrashing. I began to shiver and to weep uncontrollably, reliving every weird moment of passion Krista had brought to me, and its devastating culmination. The orgasm that seized me was as powerful as any I could recall experiencing. I was horrified. Of course I was. Yet, in the deep recesses of my mind, I felt I was reassuring myself that this was how I felt. The real shame was the way my body had participated, had responded, had burst into that shattering climax. No matter how hard I tried to tell myself that it was forced upon me, that I had no choice but to endure the whole sick episode, I could not convince myself. That was the true shame.

I had spoken the truth when I told Krista I had never made love with a girl. All I'd had were some silly teenage experiments. Yvonne, a school friend who used to stay with me, and I with her, had talked about it. Lesbianism. We couldn't even say the word without a guilty snigger. We didn't really understand it. 'I wonder what it's like?' Yvonne once pondered, and we both blushed, thinking the same thoughts, titillated by the notion of girls touching one another.

One night we pretended to be fooling, teasing, though in reality we knew we were both half serious, afraid, yet spurred on by our curiosity. We kissed. 'I'll be the boy,' Yvonne giggled. But then, with her tongue in my mouth, my own fervent responses were no joke. We strained against each other, our breasts pressing and merging and our thighs and bellies moulding, until we broke apart with tearful laughter, red-cheeked and privately aghast at the thrills we had stirred.

We never tried it again, but my waking dreams – those solitary fantasies I was helpless to prevent and which came when, gripped by shame yet driven by compulsion, I would explore and caress my naked body behind the locked bathroom door, or with thighs parted under the bedclothes – would often centre on those wicked pleasures. I imagined making love with all kinds of females, from film stars to schoolmates and teachers. Or rather, being made love to, for I was never the active one, always the passive recipient whose helpless body was brought to fruition by my beautiful temptresses.

And now it had happened – for real. And yes, I was the victim, I told myself as I wept miserably in that stinking plane. But it did not make me feel less guilty.

And then I sobbed with relief when, after what seemed a long time, Carl came back. He grunted and flung himself down beside the porthole. He didn't even look at me. I was deeply wounded. Surely he must have been concerned when I was led away? Why wasn't he clutching me to him, relieved at seeing me safe again?

Instead he slumped, his head back against the bulkhead. It was as if he did not see me. He covered his face with his hand, lost in his own despair, it seemed. I wanted to shout at him, to claw at him. The bastard! Suddenly I wanted to tell him, to scream at the selfish bastard, what had just happened to me. I flounced away from him, putting space between us, and rested uneasily on my hip, my body angled towards the aisle. At least my anger had dried my tears, and feeling physically and emotionally drained, I drifted into an uneasy doze.

'Come on, up you get. You are moving. Quickly, everyone into the aisle. Stand still.'

I stirred, heart thumping. A great leap of hope surged in me. 'What's going on now?' I blurted, blinking wearily at Carl. Even in my hope, I was startled by the ravaged lines of his face. I hardly recognised him.

'We are moving you to a new location,' the leader announced. 'We have been given permission to take you off the plane.' His English was good, his voice precise.

'Do not attempt to escape, or do anything foolish.' He held up a thick belt festooned with round, dark objects. 'We all have grenades and automatic weapons. We will commence firing immediately if anyone of you does something foolish. Most, if not all, will die, I can assure you. Now, move when we tell you to.'

We were not allowed to take any hand baggage with us. Bemused, half buoyed by renewed hope and half dismayed that there was no mention of our release, we obeyed. We filed off that plane where we seemed already to have spent a lifetime, and climbed onto a bus that waited beside the tail of the aircraft bathed in arc lights.

We set off on a slow, bumpy journey of what seemed miles. In the distance we could see the lighted airport buildings, several large jets standing before it, but we went nowhere near it. Instead we came to an isolated place, and I heard a voice whisper close behind me, 'These were the old airport buildings before they built the new extensions.'

They had been hastily prepared for us. There was dust and signs of neglect all round, except for the long bare room into which we were herded. It was an old passenger waiting lounge. We could see ourselves reflected dimly in the long glass panes. Even then I wondered why nobody came near, why there were no attempts at rescue, though coward that I am, I was glad this was so.

'It is necessary for you to split up,' Khotan announced, standing on an upturned box and aiming his gun over us. 'We must have the women in one room, the men in another. It is necessary.' There were murmurs of protest, mine among them, but we were all too dispirited and broken to argue. 'You will meet up later,' he called reassuringly, and I clung to Carl. Was it my imagination, or did he really stiffen uncomfortably in my tight embrace, just as he had on numerous other occasions recently when I had tried to instil some passion into our relationship? When I broke away, I blushed as I saw Krista's sarcastic gaze fixed on me.

She gestured with her gun. 'In there.' There were about a dozen of us women who filed through a door to find ourselves standing in a bleak ablution area, with a row of three toilet cubicles and hand basins. At one end there was a tiled recess with two showers. 'Undress,' she ordered. 'Quickly! You bitches stink like hell. You all take a shower, now!' She yelled the last word and we flinched. There were a few gasped protests, but no one refused. Though embarrassing, we were at least all female, and we shuffled swiftly out of our dirty clothes to stand self-consciously trying to hide as much of our naked bodies as we could.

The water was cold, but we did not need to be told how unsavoury we were, and we jostled to crowd under the two jets, rubbing and bumping against each other, turning under the blessed streams of water and, dignity forgotten, cleaning ourselves vigorously. Then there was a sudden gasp of shock, and the woman next to me said, 'My God! Did she do that?'

I looked blank for a second, and then saw that she, and all the others, were staring at my backside. The criss-crossed weals stood out vividly on my white skin, and still smarted at my light touch. I blushed and stammered, then heard Krista's ringing laughter. 'You see, ladies, what can happen if you are naughty,' she mocked. 'You must be good for me, yes?'

There was a pile of old but clean white towels on a bench, and we grabbed them eagerly, wrapping them about us, but Krista chuckled scornfully. 'Leave your towels here, ladies,' she said, and as she herded us towards the door in single file the snout of her gun prodded towards one of Nicky Gimburg's lovely breasts, separating her from the rest of us like a sheepdog singling out a ewe. 'You, wait,' she snapped, and Nicky stopped. 'The rest go,' Krista ordered, and we filed on, eyes downcast. 'You, Jane,' Krista called to me. 'You wait, too.'

When we were alone with her, she jerked the gun at Nicky. There was no doubting the menace in her move, or her look. 'Over there, and face the wall,' she ordered. For a second Nicky hesitated, and I jumped as Krista clicked the bolt on her weapon. 'Don't give me an excuse, slut,' she threatened. 'Now move!'

The athletic figure moved. She stood close to the grimy white tiles, her back to us. 'Why are you picking on me?' she asked over her shoulder. 'What have I done to you?'

'You have annoyed me, slut,' Krista told her. 'You need to be taught a lesson. Doesn't she, Jane? Here, tie her hands to the hooks. Spread her arms out on either side.'

Nicky's voice cracked with fear, but she made a brave effort to speak up for herself. 'You've no right to treat me like this,' she complained. 'I've done nothing to you. You can't treat me like this—'

Krista leapt forward and jabbed her gun at the naked figure. The barrel was thrust obscenely between the cheeks of Nicky's bottom, the tip penetrating the deep cleft until two hollows appeared in the rounded flesh as Nicky clenched her buttocks in fright. I prayed she would not try to fight. I saw every muscle in that wonderful frame tighten. 'Try it!' Krista invited, her tone dangerous. 'Go on, and I will enjoy crushing you!'

I sobbed in terror. 'Please, Nicky!' I pleaded. 'Just do what she says.'

'There, you see?' Krista mused. 'Jane knows how to behave.' I withered with shame, yet sighed with relief at seeing the athletic figure slump and her shoulders heave in a huge sob of defeat. Her breasts touched the cold tiles as I bound her outstretched wrists to the large metal clothes hooks that protruded from the wall at shoulder height. Krista had flung two short lengths of rope at me. Inexpert as I was, I pulled them tight before I twisted them round and round the metal, and knotted them. I winced at the thought of hurting Nicky, but was even more afraid of what might happen if she tore her arms free. For I knew, and dreaded, what was to come.

I found soon enough that I had done my job all too well. Sickened, I stood by and watched the wicked punishment Krista meted out. That leather belt was there, curled around her fist, only this time she seemed to use it with far more venom than she had wielded with me. She drew her right arm back, and struck with deliberate fury. The crack of the lash made every nerve fibre in my body tense. It curled around the writhing bottom, and sent a line of fire rippling across the centre of those exquisite flanks. Nicky jerked and her body smacked into the tiles against which she was pinioned while a scream of torment was ripped from her. I watched her shorn head threshing with pain and humiliation. The athletic frame bent and squirmed, tugging against the cords that bit cruelly into her wrists; the cords I in my craven subservience had tied. Another vicious crack fell and another searing welt appeared on the pale haunches, which dimpled deeply and swayed in a hopeless effort to escape their punishment.

Soon the blows were falling with less precision, which merely served to add to Nicky's ordeal as the leather bit into the backs of the tanned thighs, or fell across her golden back. The wicked tip of the belt curled around her hips and thighs to add further pain as it bit into the mound adorned by that sweet little blonde tuft. Her buttocks and the area around them were a livid mass of interlaced lines, as though some wild beast had clawed at her, which was no doubt how it felt to the twisting frame. Nicky was howling, begging for mercy, sagging against the ropes that held her, all thought of pride or defiance gone. She blubbered blindly in her anguish and her grief. 'Oh nuh-no! Please! Oh please! Stop! Please! I beg you!'

Krista was panting heavily when her arm fell for the last time. Her face ran with perspiration, and her breasts were heaving under the sweat-stained shirt. She moved forward, close to the sagging girl, whose body was wracked with convulsive sobs. She leaned close until her lips were brushing the girl's neck, around which she slipped her hand and held her gently by the throat. 'You see, my dear girl?' she breathed softly, sensuously. 'You have got to learn to be a good little slut, have you not...? Have you not?' she insisted, and gave the blonde head a little shake.

'Y-yes,' Nicky whispered, tears meandering down her

cheeks.

Krista kissed her behind the ear, and then let her go. 'Get the slut down,' she said to me, dismissively. 'And bathe those stripes for hers.'

She went out and I moved to pick at the bonds, which had tightened even more. It took quite a struggle to release her. There were twin circles of red around her wrists where the ropes had chafed them. She slumped down on her haunches, her shoulders bowed, her head resting against the tiles. 'Leave me alone, you cuh – creep!' she wept.

I was crying too. Gingerly, I put my hands under her arms. I couldn't have lifted her on my own, but at my touch she made the effort and stood up, groaning as she did so. 'Look, I had to do what she told me,' I protested. 'She beat me, too. You've seen my bum.' She let me lead her back to the shower stall, where she supported herself, her hands resting on the tiles, while I dabbed gently at her livid weals with a sopping towel. Her breath hissed, and those lovely rounds tautened at every contact. But at last her pain seemed to ease a little, and the violence of her weeping subsided somewhat.

She didn't demur as I held her round the waist to help her hobble back out to the main room. The showers had been left running the whole time, but they had not been enough to drown the yelps and shrieks of Nicky, and all eyes were on us. A row of thin foam mattresses had been placed along one wall, and the other girls were stretched out, huddled under the single dark grey blanket each had been given. There were two empty spaces at one end, and we moved towards them.

Then we noticed, and tried belatedly to hide our nakedness, as we saw two grinning African men handing out mugs of tea and chunks of bread. And our embarrassment was quashed momentarily as we stared in astonishment at another figure in full uniform, including a steel helmet, holding an automatic rifle and standing on guard by the doorway.

Hastily we scrambled to sit down on the mattresses and haul the blankets up over our nakedness. 'What's going on?' I asked under my breath. Nicky had taken the end space, and the girl on my other side was the pretty coloured stewardess. She was as naked as the rest of us, and was holding the blanket modestly up over her breasts.

'Our guards have been changed,' she muttered anxiously. 'Looks like President Koloba and his cohorts are in on the kidnapping. That's why it's been so easy for the hijackers.'

No one was talking much, if at all. I sat hunched miserably, trying to keep the coarse blanket from falling from my shoulders while I nibbled at the dry bread and sipped the hot, sweet tea. But I found time, despite my own worry and misery, to wonder how Carl was faring, and when, if ever, I would see him again.

Chapter Five

We remained in complete isolation for the next three days. We had no contact with the outside world, and heard nothing of the men from whom we had been separated. Of the twelve of us, there were only three who were married and whose husbands were being held too. One was a petite, delicate-looking girl, Moira Kinsella, with rich chestnut hair which hung in fluffy waves about her elfin face. She had the pale complexion that often goes with red hair, and there was a light dusting of freckles over her nose and cheeks as well as her fragile shoulders.

It soon became obvious that the Koloba regime was cooperating fully in our kidnapping, for Krista, and the three male hijackers, disappeared completely for all that time, replaced by fully accoutred native soldiers who, though they didn't touch us or attempt to communicate with us, stared appreciatively at our naked bodies as they stood on guard. We hid ourselves as much as we could, keeping to our mattresses with our blankets draped round us. It was difficult though, especially when mealtimes came, to keep our breasts covered as we ate. Looking back, I can see how useful to our captors our nudity was. Not only did it inhibit us physically, and stifle any thoughts of resistance, but it helped to demoralise us with shocking rapidity as well.

By the second day, however, we were already becoming

less concerned with hiding our nakedness, both from each other and our male guards. The lack of protective clothing helped to instil the idea of our helplessness, our worthlessness as individuals, and to accept our captivity with passive fatalism. This was all confirmed later, in many frank conversations with Krista and the others.

We got to know one another pretty well in our enforced leisure. We lay talking for hours, trying to comfort and encourage one another, revealing all kinds of intimate details of our past, things we would never have dreamt of discussing in more normal circumstances. I even found myself, while lying next to Moira sharing the thin mattress, confessing the sorry state of my marriage. The tears came quickly, and soon a comforting arm was around my shoulder as I sobbed my grief. 'He duh – doesn't seem to nuh – need me or want me any more,' I spluttered, ashamed of my disloyalty and yet needing to talk. 'Even in bed; we haven't had sex for months.' I blushed as I remembered the afternoon in the hotel. Was it really only a matter of three or four days ago? In any case, I wasn't going to go into the sad mechanics of that episode.

Of the other, single girls, two were part of the cabin crew. The pretty coloured girl was called Anita Simpson. Although, at twenty-one, she was three years younger than me and one of the youngest, except for Nicky Gimburg, who at nineteen was the baby of the group, she emerged as our leader and spokesperson, and did her best to keep our failing spirits up. She still felt she had a responsibility for us, as an employee of the airline.

And some of us gave cause for worry, particularly Nicky, who lay on her mattress in despairing silence for hours at a time. The unprovoked punishment in the shower room seemed to have a profound effect on her. The weals clearly bothered her, for she lay on her stomach and tossed off the blanket, complaining that she could not bear even its light pressure on her stinging flesh. 'Let them look,' she muttered apathetically when Anita protested that the guards could see.

I obtained permission to go to the washroom and wrung out a towel, which I brought to dab gently at the enflamed bars on Nicky's skin. 'You're not going to tie me again, are you?' she asked unfairly; it seemed she found it hard to forgive me for my part in her ordeal, even though I explained how helpless I was.

But my deepest shame was something I could not tell anyone about. As I stared at the naked bodies around me, I burned with shame at my reaction, for there was an undeniable frisson of sexual excitement deep within me. Krista's abuse of my body in the darkness had stirred something in me I had never known existed. Could it be? Was it possible I was, after all, gay?

It was with mixed emotions that I looked on her again when, after her lengthy absence, the German girl returned looking refreshed in the neatly pressed military shirt and slacks and the supple suede boots she wore. When her grey eyes met mine, I felt myself blushing ridiculously and I could not hold her look, although before I looked away I saw the dimples of a smile forming on her cheeks.

'Right, ladies,' she said. 'Stand by your beds and let me have a look at you. Up, come on, up!'

Awkwardly we stood, holding our blankets around us, and she laughed. 'No, no, we must be military, I think.

Blankets folded, and put them at the top of your beds.' We complained sulkily, but did as we were told. We stood there with our hands crossed in front of us, keenly aware of the delighted stares of the two guards stationed by the door. Krista moved down the row, stopping before each one of us, standing uncomfortably close and staring pointedly at us until there were several sniffles and muffled weeping.

When she paused in front of the athletic figure of Nicky, I held my breath and prayed. 'Turn around,' Krista ordered curtly. The toned shoulders seemed to droop, and the girl obeyed. I exhaled slowly with relief, and then heard her give a hiss of shock and discomfort as Krista traced the lines of welts running over her beaten buttocks. They hollowed and a shudder passed through the athletic frame as Krista stroked the firm rounds of flesh, following their contours, brushing her fingers lightly down the central divide, as she had with me.

'Do not worry, my little slut,' she said. 'As long as you are an obedient girl, you will not be punished any more.' The voice, deceptively gentle, as though addressing a child, added to the deep humiliation the girl was experiencing, and I was afraid again; we recognised the strength of Nicky's sculptured physique, we knew what a good athlete she was and that she wanted to make her career in sports. She was still at college, and had been heading out to Africa to spend the long summer vacation working for an aid organisation.

But the whipping had effectively curbed her natural ebullience. She stood, head bowed, the tears running down her face again, while Krista leisurely studied the evidence of her beating and then, with one last demonstrative tap on the marked bottom, moved away.

It was the lovely Anita who was the next to feel Krista's wrath. Although she looked scared, she bravely stood and faced the German after Krista had finished her inspection and was about to leave again. 'Please,' she said, her demeanour respectful. 'Can you give us any news about what is happening, and about what is going to happen? Is anything being done to negotiate our release?' She tumbled on, the words speeding up in her nervousness. 'And the men – the male hostages. When can we see them? Are they all right?'

Krista's eyebrows lifted, and she smiled. 'My, my, so many questions,' she mused. 'You sound like a politician, or a reporter. I'll give you my answer in private. And you, Jane and Nicky, you come too.' She strode off in the direction of the washroom, and we all three stared at one another in mute consternation. It was a tribute to Krista's authority, and our own subservience, that we all turned and followed her while the others gazed worriedly after us.

In the washroom, Krista commanded me to turn on the showers. I was trembling, my legs once more feeling like jelly as I obeyed. There was a bench against the wall, a low wooden thing only a foot or so high such as you see in a school gym. 'Bring it,' Krista ordered, and again we moved to obey. 'Lie down,' she said pleasantly, smiling at Anita, who stared as though hypnotised. 'You heard me – lie down. On your front.' After some hesitation, Anita moved gingerly to obey the instruction, stretching carefully along the narrow bench. 'Now, you two; Jane, you hold her wrists, and Nicky, you are strong, so you hold her ankles.'

'No,' Nicky said defiantly, shaking her head, for she knew, as we all did now, what was to happen.

But surprisingly Krista showed no sign of anger. 'Look,' she said, as though explaining something to fractious children, 'we have been discussing our mission, and some of us are quite convinced that it is time we showed that we mean business. And that means killing one or two of you. Some of my comrades are very keen to do it. Now, I would rather it was not any of you.' She chuckled. 'Yes, I admit I am being selfish,' she nodded at Nicky and me, 'because I would far prefer them to pick on the men.'

My heart turned over as my selfish terror was replaced by fear for Carl. As though reading my mind, Krista chuckled again and looked directly at me. 'And I can even put in a word for your man, Jane. As long as you are all good girls,' she added pointedly, pulling the belt from her slacks as she spoke. 'And as for you,' she turned her attention back to Anita, 'I cannot have you speaking to me disrespectfully like that in front of the others. I must have obedience and respect at all times. So, no more nonsense. Let us get on, shall we?'

We were all three crying by now. Nicky and I straddled the wooden bench and captured Anita's wrists and ankles. We gripped her tightly, for we knew that the harder her struggles, the worse the punishment would be.

Perhaps Krista was in a good mood after her period away from us, presumably giving her time for sleep and refreshment. Perhaps our submission had pleased her.

Whatever the reason, her thrashing of Anita, though painful enough, was nowhere near as venomous as that which Nicky or I had received.

She controlled her strokes carefully, bringing the belt cracking down across the girl's lovely upturned buttocks. They flexed and jerked, and red lines, which darkened rapidly, marred their smoothness. Anita's body jerked and twisted on the narrow wood, and I had to hold on tight to prevent her from pulling free. I could see the muscles tense on Nicky's arms as she also held the girl tightly in place.

As the blows fell, leaving vivid parallel lines to match the first, Anita turned her head and shrieked in torment. Krista waited after each stroke until the anguished heaving had subsided. This allowed her victim to savour the full burning throb of each lash before the next descended with a sickening thwack. Anita's bottom was cruelly aflame with the overlaid weals when the whipping was finally terminated.

My own body was coated in perspiration; it was running down between my breasts, trickling down the curve of my belly to catch in my pubes. The tears were streaming down Anita's uncomprehending features, and the angry imprints of our grip marked her wrists and ankles. When we released her, she remained where she was, her body shaking and her hands hovering behind her as she sought to alleviate the sting of her livid flesh but could not bear even her own light touch.

'Towel,' Krista commanded casually, and I moved quickly to soak the cloth in cold water and dab tenderly at the flinching buttocks. We had to help the sobbing figure upright. You could see the indentations where the bench had pressed into her breasts and her inner thighs. Nicky stooped, held her around the waist, helped her stand, and then we all moved back towards the other room.

'Wait, Jane, stay here,' Krista said.

When the others had gone, I turned and faced her, my tears still gliding down my cheeks. I was shaking, and Krista smiled at my distress. She came close, and I forced myself not to cower away from her when her palm caressed my cheek. 'I think you have learnt your lesson, Jane,' she whispered.

I nodded, and my voice would scarcely come. 'Yes, we all have,' I said truthfully. 'We don't want any trouble. The last thing we want to do is upset you.'

She gave a triumphant laugh, and then shook her head in amusement. 'No, of course you do not. You are my little chickens, are you not? But I have to teach you a lesson. I have to keep you obedient.'

'But we are obedient,' I protested. 'We'll do whatever you tell us. Please, you don't have to keep punishing us,' I ended with a sob, afraid that my very words might spark her anger off.

I needn't have worried. 'I know,' she mused. 'I am wicked, no?' Her voice dripped with sensuality. 'But I will tell you something.' Her voice dropped to the softest of whispers and her grey eyes danced with mischief. 'It gives me such a thrill to punish you. You do not know how excited it makes me, my little darling.' She sniggered like a mischievous schoolgirl. 'And now…' she put her hand lewdly over her crotch, 'my panties are so wet, my little darling.'

I dropped my gaze, shocked and thrilled by her confession. 'Come,' she whispered, her lips brushing my ear. 'You have not forgotten our little rendezvous under the plane, have you? I am sure you have not. I am sure you have been thinking about that night quite a lot.'

I could barely catch my breath my heart was hammering so hard. She flicked my right nipple, which was standing erect from its puckered surround, as was its twin. 'Yes, I see you have not forgotten out little rendezvous, my little slut,' she murmured, and gave a throaty giggle. Then she left me abruptly and went to the doorway. 'No one is to come in here until I tell you!' she called out, and I felt a red tide of shame engulf me. Now everyone would know for sure what was going on.

Krista led me to the showers. Her eyes never leaving mine, she began to undress slowly, tantalisingly, as part of her relentless seduction of me. She undid the buttons of her shirt, slipped it out from her slacks, and let it fall from her shoulders. She was wearing a khaki sleeveless vest beneath it. I should not have been surprised, yet somehow I had expected something more feminine. Underneath the light cotton, I could see the shape of her breasts, the nipples thrusting against the cloth a clear sign of her arousal. She squatted awkwardly and unlaced her boots, still staring at me. I stood motionless, except for my involuntary trembling. I could not take my eyes from her.

The boots off, she stood and shrugged down her slacks and stepped out of them. Her briefs were plain, and though cut high on the leg, they were the same drab colour as her vest. The short grey socks were thick and ugly, and yet, paradoxically, she looked extremely sexy in the graceless clothing. She pulled her vest swiftly off over her head, and shrugged down her briefs. The socks were the last to go. Her pubic hair was neatly trimmed and short, and noticeably darker than the blonde hair on her head. 'You like what you see?' she asked levelly, standing close to me but making no effort to touch me. I nodded wordlessly. 'Come, we get in the shower together,' she said.

She made me stand while she took a tablet of white soap and washed me thoroughly, all over, from my neck down to my feet, until I was coated in a lather of slippery bubbles. She took her time, her hands lingering on my breasts, and then on my tummy and my buttocks and my thighs, moving downwards. I shivered at her touch on my calves, and leaned against the cold wet tiles while she lifted first one of my feet and then the other, washing each one carefully, even parting my toes with her thumb and forefinger.

My whole body was alive with an urgent need now, so that when her hands came slowly up again, up the insides of my thighs, to move in on my curl-capped mound and the moist cleft of my sex, I ground myself against them with a whimpered cry of pleading. Our open mouths locked together and we sank down together, our limbs and bodies coiled in a fusion of lust, to writhe on the hard wet floor. Her fingers found their way into the slippery passage of my vagina, and her thumb stroked at my beating clitoris until I sobbed, begging for the release that came, surging through me with such force that my feet kicked and splashed on the wet floor, and I shuddered at the terrifying, wonderful force of the orgasm that seared through me.

'Ohhhh…' I wept, jerking against her and clinging to her as though I could force our bodies to join as one, until I was utterly spent and collapsed in her embrace. She held me to her breasts, and I felt her shiver as I suckled her nipple while she sat and rocked me back and forth with comforting tenderness, like a mother with her baby.

Chapter Six

I felt like a different person when I walked out of that shower room. For a start, Krista led me out, holding me by the hand. To me, it was a blazing proclamation of our relationship. I stared down at my bare feet, my toes curling with embarrassment. The fact that I was naked and she was dressed seemed somehow to make it worse. I blinked back the tears and crept to my space between Anita and Nicky. The dark-haired girl was lying on her stomach, her back bare and her breasts hidden by the mattress. The blanket was folded loosely about her hips, barely concealing the red marks of her beating. She was sniffling quietly. I could feel all their eyes on me, and I wished the floor would open up beneath me.

'Now you will all be good girls, you hear?' Krista announced, with a broad smile. 'That is all you have to worry about. And no more silly questions, okay?' Then she murmured something to the guards, and left.

'What is it with you and that Kraut bitch?' Nicky asked, her eyes boring into me resentfully.

'We know what it is,' someone further down sneered. 'Some people will stoop to anything, eh girls? And I mean *stoop*,' she added significantly.

The tears brimming in my eyes spilled over and I looked around me desperately. I could hardly get the words out. 'You think I want that?' I sobbed. 'Being touched up by that – that perv? I had to let her do it! You know I can't…' my shoulders heaved and I flung myself down wearily, my head cradled in my arms. There was an uneasy silence, except for the sound of my harsh sobbing. There were no more comments, but I felt their glances on me all the time after that, mistrusting and uncertain, wondering if I was telling the truth, or whether they had a traitor in their midst.

To add to my agony of shame, Krista now singled me out every time she came, beaming smiles of proprietary affection at me, ruffling my hair and throwing a casual arm over my shoulder. I wasn't totally shunned, though; I think most of them were too scared to do that, which was saddening in itself. But there were plenty of snide remarks and jokes about 'Krista's lover'.

I was touched by the way Moira Kinsella, the lovely redhead, stuck up for me. 'Look, she can't help it,' she argued vehemently one day. 'If that vicious sadist has picked on her, well…' she shrugged eloquently.

We were allowed to shower more or less whenever we wanted now. Sometimes one of the guards would poke his head in, but we had become inured to that. We found that if we just stopped and stared at them pointedly, they would usually grin sheepishly and turn away.

I found myself sharing the shower stall with Moira one hot afternoon. 'Don't take any notice of those bitches out there,' she scowled. Then she gave a dirty little snigger. 'I bet they're just jealous, don't you think?' We were standing close together, our shoulders brushing under the tepid stream. 'I don't think it's that bad, anyway,' she went on. 'I mean, girls making out with each other. I've often thought, well, that I wouldn't mind trying it...' she let her voice trail away and ran her fingers down my arm from my shoulder to my elbow, letting her nails scratch softly over my skin. I shivered responsively.

She turned around, away from me, but she stayed so close that I felt her bottom brush against the tops of my thighs. 'Do my back for me,' she murmured, holding the piece of rag that served as a washcloth over her shoulder. Having the sexy little creature so close to me, so temptingly close, I found it increasingly hard to catch my breath.

'But, um, they'll all gossip about us,' I managed to protest shakily.

She gave that salacious little chuckle again. 'Let them,' she shrugged with a delightfully carefree innocence. 'And if they're going to gossip anyway, let's give them something to *really* talk about.'

So I caressed her with the soap, beginning gingerly to move the cloth over her dainty shoulders and then down the hollow of her slim back to that little divided bottom, no bigger than a boy's. Then suddenly, she seized my wrist and stepped back into me, so that my front was pressed against her. She moved my hand under her right arm, and placed it over one of her breasts. I passed the cloth over it, and felt her clenching bottom rubbing intimately at my belly and thighs. My knuckles brushed against her tiny nipple, and I could feel that it was rubbery, fully erect. Then somebody bustled in and I reluctantly sprang back guiltily. But the newcomer headed straight for one of the toilets. 'Sorry,' she called, 'but I've got another dose of the shits!'

Moira was facing me now, leaning back impishly against

the tiles. She lifted her head, and her darkened red hair streamed like seaweed about her pale face and shoulders. Her violet eyes held me with an unspoken message I was, for some reason, frightened to read. So instead I hastened away from her, grabbing my towel and wrapping it tightly around me.

But later, in the oppressively humid darkness, lying with the rough blanket down to my waist, my thoughts were a riotous tumble. I relived the feel of that pale breast under my hand, the brush of its tiny nipple… and the feel of that other nipple, scarcely any bigger, in my mouth as I suckled in the arms of Krista. I relived every touch until I was shaking, and I couldn't keep my fingers from straying down to my tufted loins to stroke and tease that moist crevice which flowered, opening, its lips engorged until I was running with my need.

I waited, partly in dread and partly in quivering anticipation, for Krista to make another move. When several days passed and she didn't single me out except for that public demonstration of favour towards me, I was shocked at my disappointment. She did not spend very much time with us now, she merely looked in on us every morning, and then once in the early evening. We were guarded entirely by the natives of the country we were being held in. We saw no sign of the other kidnappers, and we were too afraid to raise any more questions about the male hostages, or about anything else at all. We tried to work out how long we had been held prisoner. It was surprising how difficult it was to keep track of time. Our watches had been removed the day after we were brought off the plane.

We each had our own biological clocks within us, though – another source of painful embarrassment in our present depleted circumstances, and one that *did* entail our humble pleas to an amused Krista – and eventually we could calculate that it was seventeen days since our seizure.

'It feels more like seventeen months,' someone said ruefully, and sighed with longing.

'More like seventeen years, you mean,' someone else added fervently.

Then one morning, Krista came in and declared, 'You girls must get some exercise. You must keep yourselves in shape. Look at you.' We certainly didn't need to worry about gaining weight. We had all lost weight, some of us noticeably. The diet, though not meagre in quantity, was depressingly unappetising. Lots of coarse bread, heaps of badly cooked rice, and gristly, stringy meat whose origin we dared not speculate on. There was a little fruit, water, and weak, milky tea to drink. It was true we needed exercise; we spent almost all our time lounging on our mattresses. After all, there was little else to do besides shower.

The room, with its concrete floor, was entirely bare with no furniture of any kind, and it was quite chilly at night. In the daytime, however, it was stiflingly hot, the sun pouring in through the long windows which lined one wall and through which we could see an empty stretch of tarmac, and then that tall, waving yellow grass. We were forbidden to go anywhere near the windows. We had no reading matter, nothing to occupy us except each other. That was why we learnt about each other so quickly.

'You must do these exercises every morning from now

on.' Under the amused grins of the guards, Krista made us line up in front of our mattresses, and put us through a routine of stretching, bending, and jogging on the spot that soon had a number of us puffing and blowing, our breath rasping painfully.

After two or three press-ups, most of us collapsed on our tummies, helpless as landed fish. Only Nicky, her body still looking splendidly in shape despite the last three weeks or so, kept going. Suddenly, the atmosphere became noticeably tense, the rest of us lying there panting heavily and watching as the wonderful physique pumped up and down, her muscles rippling and standing out under her still-golden tan – and the fading stripes of the beating, which marked her paler behind as it dipped and lifted and the rounds dimpled and clenched like a beautiful living statue.

'Keep going!' Krista challenged, and lovely Nicky did, her face growing redder and dripping with perspiration, the cords in her neck standing out. It was a long while before she collapsed with a great gasp, and lay with her face touching the floor, her whole body quivering.

'Well done!' Krista cried gleefully. 'You see?' She turned to the rest of us. 'Aren't you all ashamed to be so feeble? Now, on your backs – let's give you a little thrill to finish, yes?' Nicky did not move, and Krista paid her no attention. She made us lift our legs with our knees locked vertically in the air. I felt my tummy muscles straining like overstretched violin strings in protest, and moaned at the effort. Then she made us open our legs wide and lower them slowly to the floor, keeping them stiff and straight all the while. You can guess what a view this gave her, a view she gave every evidence of enjoying as she made us repeat the manoeuvre nine more times, as slowly as we could.

She came and stood in front of me as I made the groaning effort for the last time, and she caught my ankles as I raised them high. She parted them, held my legs open, and I relaxed, letting her warm hands take the strain. Looking up at the dominant woman, I shamefully felt an excited pulsing in my vagina, and felt the oily secretion of desire in the cleft that was so mercilessly opened to her. She put her booted foot very gently on my mound, over my dark triangle, and pressed lightly, rolling the cushioned pad of flesh under her sole in a circular motion, and the muscles of my inner thighs tightened as I bit my lower lip. She felt my movement and smiled broadly as my eyes stared up at her, filled with tears.

'What a charming sight,' she murmured. Her wicked lips pursed and blew a kiss, and then she released my ankles and left the room.

'Why don't you ask her what's going on?' someone demanded pointedly when she had gone. 'What's being done to get us out of here?'

I blushed deeply. 'I can't,' I said defensively. 'You know what she's like – what she's already done.' My hand gestured towards my bottom, but my challenger snorted a derisive laugh and shook her head.

'Yes, but that was before,' she went on. 'Now you're clearly her favourite, so you might as well put your talents to some use. I mean for all of us, as well as for yourself.'

'Don't be so stupid,' Moira countered on my behalf. 'You know it's not Jane's fault Krista picked on her. Just be thankful Jane can make a difference. She hasn't beaten anyone since Anita, has she? Believe me, if Jane can keep her sweet, it's good for all of us.' Moira slipped an arm around my waist as she made this spirited defence, and though I was grateful for the support, it did not ease my discomfort at the situation I unwittingly found myself in, especially when I saw my attacker give a conspiring sideways glance at those near her.

That evening, we had already finished our simple meal and one of the guards had cleared away the dishes and departed before Krista reappeared. As usual, she wore her military-style shirt and slacks.

'Come with me,' she said, pointing at Nicky, and then without another word she turned and strode towards the door through which she had entered.

Nicky rose, clutching the blanket loosely around her chest. 'But why?' Her voice betrayed her anxiety. She glanced round at the rest of us, seeking support. 'What do you want me for? Where are you taking me?'

Krista turned, her face showing only a mild expression of surprise. 'I beg your pardon?' she said. 'What on earth has that got to do with you?' She came back to the row of mattresses, and Nicky nervously lifted the blanket higher. 'I thought you had learnt by now.' The voice was still soft, perfectly poised. 'You simply do as you are told. You of all people should know that, slut.'

Nicky's blue eyes were wide with trepidation. 'I've told you before,' she said with little conviction, 'I am not a slut.' Then she pulled her shoulders back with as much defiance as she could muster. 'And I have rights. We all have rights. We're not animals. Keeping us like this is not acceptable. Keeping us naked, with those wretched men leering at us the whole time.' She fell silent, and suddenly seemed to realise that she'd perhaps made a big mistake. Doubt could now be seen in her eyes and her posture.

Krista shook her head and said, 'No, have I not made it clear by now that you have no rights?' she asked, almost sounding reasonable. 'You have no rights at all. You have no tights at all,' she repeated. 'You belong to us now, and we do whatever we like with you. You are our property.' She smiled. 'And a very desirable property, too.' She shook her head again, this time with a gesture of impatience, and moved right up close to Nicky, who visibly tensed. 'I guess you think you are a big girl now, no?' Krista said with sudden vehemence. 'Maybe you think I am afraid of you, no?'

Nicky looked round at us, her eyes seeking help – but there was none forthcoming.

'I do not need the guards, baby,' Krista went on, 'or even a gun, to make you obey me at all times.' She pushed her face within inches of Nicky's, who had to lean back slightly. 'Come on,' Krista challenged softly, totally composed as she held up her hands in invitation. 'Drop the blanket. We've all seen you naked. Show us how tough you are, yes?' She reached out, snatched the blanket out of Nicky's grasp, and tossed it aside. 'Come on, let's see you thrash me... slut.'

With a convulsive sob and a scream, Nicky launched herself at her tormentor, her hands raised to grab her by the throat. But Krista swayed away with ease, her right arm came back a little, and she drove a short but vicious punch into Nicky's midriff just at the base of her ribcage.

There was a soft thud, and I heard the cutting off of air, followed by a muffled gasp as Nicky folded, her hands dropping to clutch at the agony that exploded in her gut. As she fell, there was another sickening crunch when Krista's other first slammed up and caught the girl on the jaw, sending the cropped golden head snapping back.

The force of the vicious blow spun Nicky sideways and she fell heavily, her legs crumpling beneath her. Those two cruel blows, punches delivered at bewildering speed and with cruel force, were enough to end the confrontation, and I remembered the clenched fist that had struck Carl in the mouth.

Nicky was wheezing and gagging, her body folded on the floor, but Krista was not about to let it end there. She bent and seized the girl under one arm, but even she had to struggle to lift the dead weight. Clearly one or both punches had knocked Nicky near senseless. She looked utterly incapable of moving, let alone standing by herself.

'Jane,' Krista panted, 'come here and help me.'

Without thinking, I hastened forward. I stooped to wedge my shoulder beneath Nicky's other arm, and between us we dragged and lugged the sack-like body to the door, and through it.

We were in a corridor. Only a few yards from me was a glass double door through which I could see the grey of the short twilight. The dark shapes of two sentries showed up through the glass. An armed guard stood at a door directly opposite the one we had passed through, and it occurred to me that on the other side of it might be the men – including my husband.

'Up the stairs.' The snapped words drew me from my

brief speculation. Feet trailing and bumping up the concrete steps, Nicky slumped between us gasping for air and moaning incoherently. Her chin was sunk against her chest. By the time we got to the top of the short flight of stairs, my own breath was nearly as noisy as the poor girl's from the strain of supporting her, and my naked body was gleaming with perspiration. Krista, too, was struggling a little as we staggered along another corridor, then through a door to the left.

We were in a room that was plainly but smartly furnished, though I had no chance to take stock of it until we had dragged our burden the last yard or two to a single bed, and dropped her gratefully onto its protesting springs.

It felt weird to be standing naked in such normal surroundings. I could see my pale reflection in the dressing table mirror. Even the contact of the rug under my feet was strange. But I had little time to think on such things. There was a long dark swelling along the line of Nicky's jaw. Her limbs stirred feebly and her head rolled back and forth on the pillow as awareness, and pain, slowly returned.

Meanwhile, Krista was busily rummaging in the top drawer of the dresser, flinging aside articles of clothing. She turned, with several belts clutched in her hand. By the time Nicky was fully conscious once more, both her wrists and ankles were securely trussed to the top and bottom of the bed's metal frame. Not that I think the bonds were necessary, that she would, or could, have put up any resistance. The fight had literally been knocked out of her. She cried quietly, her anxious gaze fixed on her aggressor, who now turned to me with a grim smile. She nodded towards a wooden chair by one wall.

'I had intended for this to be a private moment, but I suppose we need have no secrets, Jane. Sit there, don't move, and don't make a sound. Understood?'

I nodded, and hastened to obey.

Very slowly and deliberately, just as she had with me in the showers, Krista began to undress, slipping off her boots, shirt, slacks, and grey socks. This time, she kept on the olive underwear of vest and knickers while the defeated girl watched impotently. Krista sat on the edge of the narrow bed beside a pinioned limb, and stroked the thigh, whose muscle tensed beneath the tormenting touch. 'I know your problem, slut,' she crooned in that gloating, sensual tone which made me shiver as I sat there holding my breath. My knuckles were white on the sides of the chair. Its unyielding wooden seat pressed into the softness of my bottom. I sat with my feet together, squeezing my thighs, feeling the increasing beat of my roused sex. 'You are used to being in control, to being the dominant one, no? You like women, I know you do, but you like them to be wetting their panties for you. And you like to get into those panties, don't you? I have known this from the first time I saw you. I am right, yes?'

Nicky was shivering, and I could see her lips trembling. 'No,' she whispered, shaking her head miserably. 'Please, leave me alone.'

'Oh, but I cannot, you know that,' Krista teased. Her hand was moving, passing over the planes and curves of Nicky's body – her thighs, the taut hollow of her stomach, that tiny patch of blonde hair between her legs, then up to the delineated shape of her ribcage, and finally, to those sweet, vulnerable breasts. Fingers plucked and teased at her nipples, which filled and pouted and swelled, a rich dark red, throbbing with helpless arousal. Feather light, the fingers trailed down again slowly, and passed over the prominence of her mound into the moist softness of the labial divide, the lips of her sex. Nicky shivered convulsively. Her hips lifted and a great sob shook her bound frame before she subsided with a desolate cry, and her thighs fell slackly open to the assault.

Krista bent triumphantly and kissed that magnificent beauty, moving from Nicky's mouth and throat down over the trembling flesh her hands had just claimed, and Nicky whimpered softly, her eyes closed, tears squeezing beneath her lids to run and dissolve into her shorn temples. The fingers of Krista never ceased their slow exploration of her prey's vulva, whose spongy tissue swelled and parted and grew wet with the hunger being remorselessly stirred. The golden tufted belly was soon lifting rhythmically again, the buttocks clenching and relaxing in time to the amorous invader.

The fingers, glistening wet, coated with flowing emissions and making soft suckling sounds, pressed further, through the outer surfaces to the evermore richly gleaming tunnel leading to the narrow vagina. They found unerringly the enflamed clitoris among the upper folds, and the heaving of the belly increased, until the springs of the bed squeaked and even Nicky's rasping moans came and went in time with this stimulation. Her hands twisted in the makeshift bonds, her feet too arched and flexed, her toes curling, as her whole body wriggled in the storm of sensations coursing through her.

Yet again Krista's lips closed over the upturned mouth, which opened and yielded blindly to the thrusting tongue. 'That is good?' Krista whispered, as their lips remained touching.

'Please… please…' whimpered the transformed girl, her body arching, rising from the bed, begging to be taken to release.

'You are nearly coming, are you not?' Krista whispered again, and Nicky shuddered.

'Oh, help me,' she mumbled. 'Yes, yes!'

'But there is more, my baby.' Krista straddled her, then slithered down, trailing her own wet sex over the writhing body beneath her until she was kneeling between the parted, tethered ankles. Her blonde head dipped, her face covered the uplifted loins, and I heard the slurping as her tongue and lips, and those nipping teeth, devoured the streaming cleft of Nicky's sex. It could not last long, that height of stimulation, and Nicky cried out, a long wail of lost ecstasy. Her body gave one emphatic heave that lifted the figure glued to her belly, and then her body slumped and shuddered as the aftershocks of the mighty orgasm spasmed through her.

I gasped, bit painfully at my lip, and convulsed in the flood of my own coming, staring down as though in amazement at the hand clasped between my thighs, the heel of the palm pressing hard against my sex, which thrust back like a lover's kiss. I was very wet; I could feel the discharge on my inner thighs and on the seat beneath me. I sank back weakly, listening to the desolate weeping from the outstretched figure, and my own tears ran unchecked for both of us, for our helplessness. Even our own bodies were treacherously triumphant over us.

I thought that was the end. I thought there could not possibly be more, but I was wrong. Krista stood, went over to the tiny shower room that adjoined her bedroom, and washed her hands at the corner basin. She pushed down her briefs, and then stripped the vest off over her head. Her body was shining with sweat, just like ours. She went to the drawers and drew out a long box. 'I must have *my* satisfaction, too,' she mused, and I gaped as I watched her step into a light harness with dark leather straps that fitted about her hips, one passing invisibly through the tight cleft of her bottom. A small leather shield fitted over her loins, following the curve of her vulva like a cache-sexe. And from the centre of this jutted a long, curving object of shining black plastic. It was about the size of a large banana, and very similar in shape. My horrified brain told me that this was a dildo. The first I had seen, apart from coloured pictures in a mail order magazine I had once shamefully and avidly studied. It did not attempt to copy the shape of a penis. There was no helm, and no imitation, veined column. Just that black, shiny smoothness, tapering and curving upward like a rhino's horn.

'Have you ever used one of these?' she asked, my whirling mind registering the weirdness of the conversation. I realised she was not addressing me, but Nicky, who was still too far gone in her reaction to what had already been done to her to be really aware of what was happening.

Receiving no audible response, Krista stood, legs astride,

and lifted the dildo, handling it with both hands, moving it so that its base rubbed against her loins. I saw her buttocks, outlined by the two dark straps that swept upward to her waist, hollow deeply.

She stooped and untied Nicky's ankles, and red marks showed where the belts had chafed. 'You'll need those long legs of yours free,' she crooned, and lowered herself slowly onto the sleek, supine body. Nicky mumbled and rolled her head in denial, but it was too late. Her arms were still fastened securely and Krista had her thighs parted wide, hooked over her arms as she knelt between them and guided the tip of the dildo to Nicky's glistening sex. It nuzzled and slid in, and Nicky moaned incoherently again. Instinctively her legs rose, knees bending, and she gripped the body on top of her with her thighs. The instrument slid deeply home, sinking into the furthermost depths of her vagina, forcing Nicky to strive to open herself yet wider to her assailant, and to lie there, wracked with the humiliation, and pleasure, while above her Krista bucked and ground, caught in the savage splendour until the explosion of her orgasm brought the bizarre coupling to its end.

Chapter Seven

Some weeks later, as soon as breakfast of lukewarm porridge and fruit was over, Nicky, Anita, Moira and myself were called out and told to report upstairs to Krista's room. It had become familiar to all four of us in the past days, both as a place of dread, and of shameful, perverse pleasures.

'There goes Krista's harem,' someone muttered, and though we blushed we said nothing, for it was true. She had used each one of us at various times for her own gratification, and had thereby taught us much about our own make-up and personality, shameful facts which we were all still trying to come to terms with.

The corridor was filled with the fresh morning sunlight; it highlighted our bodies as we walked nervously up the stairs. We hardly noticed the lecherous stares of the soldiers now, or their lewd grins and comments which, fortunately for us, we could not understand.

In Krista's room, laid out on her bed, were four sets of clothing, or rather, four dresses, all identical. They were made of thin white cotton, and had unattractive square-cut sleeves, which came to just above our elbows. The neck was square too, and modestly high. The hems reached our knees, and they fell in a straight sheath, but of so generous a width that they hid our body shape beneath. Except for Nicky, for they were all the same size, so that hers reached only to mid-thigh, and the cloth was stretched tight across her bust, showing the shape of her splendid breasts. There was the shadowy hint of her areolae, with the shape of her nipples standing out, for we were given no underclothes.

'Oh *my*,' Krista breathed appreciatively, and gave the swelling rounds a playful poke. 'You could make anything look sexy, my Viking maiden.' Recently her attitude towards Nicky had changed completely. As, indeed, had Nicky's towards her, for she took everything with a fatalistic acquiescence, which saddened me, even while it brought a measure of relief. As for the rest of us, our garments looked like shapeless hospital gowns, and were equally unflattering. For footwear we wore simple rubber sandals – flip-flops.

Wearing clothes again, even these ugly dresses, felt strange, the sensation of the material rubbing our bodies oddly titillating. But as usual we were far too edgy to worry for long about our appearance, even though Krista gave us brushes and combs and insisted we tidy our unkempt hair. There was even a little make-up, which we applied crowding round the dressing table mirror, under Krista's critical appraisal. 'You will have to do,' she decided, after a few minutes. 'Now come along with me.'

Next door, in an almost identical room, we were presented to Khotan, the leader of the hijackers, who was apparently waiting for us, and I for one experienced an acute self-consciousness, and I felt myself blushing furiously, smoothing out the dress and patting my hair. He was the first man we had seen, apart from our anonymous guards, for two months.

The first thing he did was to reiterate the warnings Krista had already given us. 'Your loved ones' and friends' lives are in your hands,' he told us. For some reason his cold eyes sought me out, adding to my befuddled thoughts and reactions. 'And I can tell you that at this moment, all of them are safe and well, including your men,' he added meaningfully. 'So it is the duty of each of you to make sure you keep them that way. Now, do exactly what you are told when we go. Do nothing to cause alarm, to us or to the people who are waiting to see you.'

Outside the room were the two other hijackers. They were carrying their automatic weapons, and I noted that Krista and Khotan had armed themselves as well. We climbed into the back of a canvass covered, camouflaged Land Rover, the driver of which looked like a Leontondese army man, and he had an armed companion in front with him.

We could not see anything of where we were going, but we drove for half an hour or more, sometimes through quite busy traffic. Our captors sat with us, and I could see that the two who wielded less authority than Khotan or Krista, in particular were tense. Their knuckles showed white as they gripped their guns. No one spoke at all during the trip.

By the time the vehicle drew to a halt, my heart was racing again. Krista's hand fell heavily on my knee, and her fingers dug into my bare skin. 'Remember, be positive in everything. Your husband's comfort, maybe his life, depends on it.' Though her words were to me, everyone heard and took note of them.

The next hour was an unreal nightmare. For a start,

there was the shock of being shepherded into a building and a room to find more than a dozen strangers facing us, and then to find myself staring up at the features of the fabled General Koloba, about whom so many fearful rumours had circulated recently in the world press. He was a giant of a man, his girth offset by his height of well over six feet. His face was broad, with the deep blackness of the northern tribes, and the triple cicatrices of tribal markings on each cheek. His eyes were small in that expanse of flesh, and their outer area was a smoky yellow. They were chillingly, compelling eyes, and I felt trapped and helpless while he held my hand in his great paw for what seemed an inordinate amount of time. I was aware of many things – of a certainty that he knew of my nakedness beneath the cotton shift, and that he could see into my spinning inner thoughts and knew the shameful truth about me.

Next came the unbelievable irony of meeting a smooth, neatly dressed official from the British Embassy, and his American counterpart. There were several cameramen, flashes popped, and at least two reporters held video recorders. These people were part of the outside world, and they would be leaving here to go back to the comforts of that outside world just as soon as they chose to, leaving us behind to our captivity. I could scarcely believe it. I had seen the evening news all my adult life. I would never have imagined it possible that one day I would find myself on the wrong side of the television glass, an actual living part of one of those terrible stories that only ever happened to other people in other parts of the world, not to people like me.

Krista and her three colleagues were standing at the back of the room, carefully out of range of the cameras, whose operators must have had strict instructions not to film them. Surely our captors would not dare to open fire in here, in front of the watching world? And surely they would not carry out their threat to murder those they still held back at the airport? These thoughts buzzed in my mind, and my stomach churned nauseatingly while we fumbled through the questions asked of us.

'Are you being treated humanely?'

'Yes,' we muttered in chorus.

'Are you speaking of your own free will?'

'Is everyone alive and well?'

We went on mumbling our affirmatives, our eyes lowered.

'Are these the clothes you normally wear?'

Suddenly the tension heightened. Anita gave a kind of gasp, her voice hurried and breathless. 'We aren't... we don't...'

The booming bass laughter of President Koloba rang out over the hesitation. 'You do not need clothes in our climate, hey? In the bush our people still go naked. By choice! No winter woollies here!' The moment had passed. Anita sank back, head down, struggling hard not to break into tears. And so, shabbily, anything to avoid later retribution, we lied our way through the press conference, or whatever it was, the feeling of unreality not only persisting but deepening. It didn't seem possible that as a result of all these flashes, and the insect-like camera lenses turned on us like guns, that our pictures would be projected around the globe.

The president moved and placed himself in the middle of us, his arms flung protectively over our shoulders. 'Do not worry, they are quite safe with me,' he declared, but his booming laughter and bear-like hug did not fool us. We knew that he was undoubtedly aligned with our kidnappers. But we trooped out obediently in his wake, not without a terrible sinking feeling that somehow we might have missed our opportunity to escape.

It was not until we had climbed back into the covered Land Rover and it had set off once more that we realised none of the hijackers was with us, and that our only sentry in the back was one of Koloba's impassive soldiers. We had not been travelling for more than two or three minutes when the vehicle halted, and we stared at one another in fresh consternation as we scrambled down over the tailboard. I had time for a fleeting glimpse of stretches of neat green lawn, punctuated by flowerbeds, then lines of tall, dark-foliaged trees. Beyond them the Great Lake was a dazzle that hurt the eyes in the fierce sunlight. The building whose broad steps we were climbing was of imposing grey stone, and though not more than two storeys high, it stretched out extensively on both sides of the pillared entrance.

Then we were inside, in a vast reception room whose polished wooden floor shone like a mirror. A man, dressed exotically in a long white gown with a broad blue sash at his waist, a short black waistcoat, and sporting a red fez, motioned for us to follow him, and we squeaked our way across the floor in our rubber sandals, the heavy boots of the soldier clomping after us. We ascended a wide red-carpeted staircase, walked down a lengthy landing, and were ushered into a room where the brightly flowered carpet, the dark furniture and heavy drapes at the long row of tall windows together with two ornate crystal chandeliers hanging centrally over the impressively long table, created an atmosphere of obscene luxury.

We were standing and staring at the room's decadent magnificence when a door at the farthest end of the lush space opened, and the bulky figure of General Koloba entered, followed by three other men in military uniform, clearly senior officers of some sort.

'Welcome to my humble little palace, ladies!' he boomed, and let out that roar of laughter of his again that was already sounding horribly familiar to me. 'A little different from your quarters, I think?' But there was that glint in those cold eyes, which made our opulent surroundings seem all the more sinister. 'But please, do not hide yourselves behind those ugly dresses. Let us see the tasty white meat we have in store for us.' The blunt words struck us like blows and we gaped stupidly at him, until he went on with mock patience, 'You want some assistance, perhaps? Shall I call for my guards to give you a hand?' Gasping, unable to hide our distress, we hastened to obey him and pulled the simple white dresses up over our heads. He gestured, and we dropped them on the floor behind us. Then we just stood there, as awkward as we would have before the humiliation of our prolonged captivity, feeling as embarrassed as we would have felt under normal circumstances had we suddenly been told to strip naked before strangers.

'Stand up straight, hands at your sides and chests out!' He commanded, and then chuckled to himself. He lined us up like recruits for his army, and he and his three cohorts advanced slowly, staring intently at each one of us, studying our trembling forms from head to toe while we stood, backs straight, clenched fists against our thighs, exactly as we had been ordered to do.

He stopped before Nicky with a low growl of lust. Inches taller than the rest of us, and fuller of figure, she clearly met with his approval, and he began a stream of comments in his own language which had his subordinates roaring in time with his own great bellows of mirth.

'This one is mine!' he declared. 'She is beautiful – like the ancient warriors.'

Then, to our utter amazement, all four men began to peel off their clothes, laying them on the couches that lined the walls, until they were as naked as we were. Their bodies' hues varied from the velvety black of Koloba and one of his officers, also of impressive size, to the almost golden-brown shade of the youngest and slimmest looking of the men, who was clearly from a different tribe.

It was a surreal scene, this luxurious room, suggestive of dignified state occasions or important conferences, with the noon sunshine pouring in through the long windows, in oblong shafts filtered by the fine mesh of the net curtains draped over the squared panes, playing over the eight naked bodies, black and white. Koloba's belly thrust out, drum-like, its grossness modified by his height and the muscled columns of his stout arms and thighs. He did not look fat in spite of that jutting paunch, though his squat, mushroom-coloured prick, hidden coyly in its shroud of foreskin, beneath the insignificant black scrub of pubis, looked oddly diminished and vulnerable. Far more impressive was the penis of the slightest, paler-skinned individual who made immediately for me and seized my wrist possessively. His prick was already rising, arching out from his bushier loins, the reddish tip of the helm showing and glistening with moisture at its slit.

Just then there was a piercing shriek that stopped everybody in their tracks. Nicky was struggling against Koloba's insistent grip, and I remembered her tortured confession to me that she was still a virgin – at least as far as men were concerned. I wanted to cry out to help her, but cowardice sealed my lips. In her panic, she really fought him, forgetting all the hard lessons she had learned during her captivity, and for a few seconds the president, giant of a man that he was, looked as though he would not be able to control her. But his great features lit up with genuine delight at the depth and passion of her struggles, and he ducked his massive shoulder into her and fastened his arms around her waist, turning his head in towards her breasts to escape her flailing blows. He heaved her off her feet like a wrestler, and with a roar of triumph, he carried her several yards to slam her down on the polished surface of the stately table with force enough to expel the air from her in an audible grunt. Before she could recover, he rolled her round onto her front and captured one of her wrists. He bent her arm wickedly up behind her, forcing her hand up between her shoulder blades until she squealed in agony and her resistance crumbled as suddenly as it had begun.

'Now, my girl,' he puffed, clearly in great good spirits, enjoying this sport immensely, 'we must teach you obedience once and for all.' With great agility for a man his size, he bent over and with his free hand snatched up one of our discarded flip-flops from the floor. Then, keeping Nicky's right arm imprisoned at her back, he brought down the light rubber sole with a mighty crack across her bottom. Again she screamed as the fiery shape stood out vividly on the quivering round, and her long legs kicked out helplessly. But, doubled as she was over the gleaming surface, she could do little but endure the blistering beating he gave her until both cheeks of her bottom were glowing hotly and she was howling like a naughty teenager, begging for mercy.

The rest of us watched motionless, caught up in the wickedly stirring spectacle, even though it lasted no more than a couple of minutes. When the president let the sandal fall from his hand, his penis was standing out stiffly, its dome-shaped head thrusting from its thick collar of foreskin. 'To work, gentlemen!' he cried, with a great guffaw, and turning his quarry over once more onto her back, he seized her statuesque thighs and parted them about his mighty hips. Nicky's cries were much more muted now, punctuating her sobs, and her only movements were in response to his driving plunges as, without further ceremony, he thrust deep into her sex.

But now, like the others, I too was preoccupied with what was happening to my own flesh. The slim figure pulled me towards one of the plush ornate crimson couches with its scrolled arms. He sat, his knees parted, and his hands dug painfully into my shoulders and neck as he pushed me down on the floor to kneel between his thighs. 'What is your name?' He asked, smiling at me, and I noticed how even and white his teeth were against his brown skin. He had a thin line of a moustache along his upper lip, and there was a swirl of hair between his nipples and a thicker bush fanning out from the base of his penis, which now jutted up at me. And I could see the fine individual hairs that covered his balls, spreading out on the rounded plush surface at the forward edge of the couch only inches from my face.

'Jane,' I whispered meekly, staring at his genitals, at their rampant grace, and imbibing the yeasty smell of his roused manhood. I knew exactly what he was going to make me do.

'Jane...' he mused. 'Well, Jane, you are very sexy, with a very sexy mouth. So be sensible, and put it to good use.'

I shuddered, as always feeling that unique mixture of terror and thrill in those seconds before I submitted to the demands of another. My lips pressed against that rearing head, and gently I let it rub against me, caressing it with my nose and cheeks and brow, until I could feel his juice smearing over my skin, and I breathed in deeply the heady aroma of him. I pursed my lips and gave a feather light kiss to that rearing column, just below the head, on the satin smoothness of the shaft. It leapt to my touch, and I felt my own muscles spasm in my moist sex. There was a sudden heady rush of pure sensuality as I told myself I was this man's slave, an object with which he could do anything he chose. I was a slave he could order to perform any act, no matter how debasing, and I must obey him, unquestioningly and without hesitation, or suffer the consequences. This was a man I had never met before, but who now, for the next few minutes, or hours, or even days, owned me. I stretched my mouth open humbly, paying homage, and took his shining helm inside me.

It swelled, and I tasted the tangy flavour of his seeping fluid, and then I gasped as he drove it deeper inside me. Or was it that I moved my stretched lips down the throbbing shaft? Maybe it was both. I'm not sure, all I know is that I sucked hard, my cheeks hollowing and my nostrils flaring. My throat worked convulsively and for a moment I gagged, fighting to breathe, and dragged my lips up the column to the swell of that head, letting my teeth graze lightly over the flange, keeping my lips against its velvety dome as I drew in blessed air, before stretching my lips wide once more and plunging the wet warmth of my cocooning mouth over his pulsing sword of flesh. Down I dove, my nose tickled by the rasping black curls of his pubes, then up again until the tip of his penis was playing over my lips, my teeth gently nibbling. My fingers caressed the base of the rearing column, felt the damp softness of his scrotum, and I panted, taking in air, lapping with greedy slurps of my tongue up the underside of his erection to where the tiny V marked the spot where the foreskin joined the helm.

I shivered with the fear and the desire that he would come inside my mouth, knowing that I would not be able to stop that instinctive jerking away from that awesome deluge of thick semen. And the subsequent frantic, open-mouthed rush to make amends for my failure by devouring every pumping drop I could lap up, or take over my proffered features. But it was not to be this time.

With a gasp, he seized my hair, and with painful force

dragged me up from his lap. At the same time, he lifted me bodily. The world spun crazily, his arms were under me, and I was being turned, I felt the couch beneath me, my shoulders and neck jammed awkwardly against its high back, my buttocks and gaping thighs raised high, his wiry body between them. Now it was he who knelt where I had and I felt his penis nuzzle, slide possessively along my soaking groove, exploring the divide of my labia, claiming it, before he nuzzled further, opening me with his potent strength, prising now the inner surfaces, entering me properly. My vagina throbbed in its frenetic welcome, closed about him, spasming in exquisite torment, and I lifted my hips imploringly, invitingly, and sighed with need and fulfilment as he drove home to the full.

We both cried out, rutting, clashing, wanting more and more, deeper and deeper until he exploded, and I came too, my body lifting in its rapturous oblivion, while all about me the air rang with similar cries as my companions in misfortune reached the peak of their own bodily nirvanas.

Chapter Eight

'How are you feeling, honey?' Anita's voice was warm with concern, her touch gentle as she laid her hand on Nicky's arm. They were standing in the tiled, glass-screened shower recess under the wonderfully soothing warmth of the powerful jets, in the gleaming bathroom to which the same servant as before had led us.

Moira and I had just vacated the shower, and were drying ourselves on the large bath towels provided for us. On the shelf over the ornate basin, with its gold-plated taps, stood row upon row of perfumes and colognes, fragrant talc and scented skin lotion. After the primitive communal existence we had known for the past couple of months, this was like some dream of heaven. Except that we had already paid a price for its luxury, as our freshly cleaned but sexually weary bodies testified.

We had not spoken, had not looked at one another as, recovered from the weird coupling in that exotic setting, we had followed the servant, leaving those four naked men and the booming laughter of General Koloba ringing in our ears. I was still bemused, for I was savouring the shockingly pleasant, enervating sensation that came after shatteringly fulfilling sex. And all with a man whose name I did not even know!

Now, shamefully intrigued and diverted from my own painful reflections by Anita's question, I listened to

Nicky's faltering reply. She too sounded dazed; as well she might after all that had happened. 'It – it wasn't too – not as terrible as I thought it – I mean the pain – it wasn't...' she shook her head in frustration, and I was startled by the vindictive words that came from the dainty figure beside me. Swathed in a towel, her red hair hanging in curling profusion about her elfin face, Moira gave a sarcastic bark of laughter.

'Hah! I should think not. I could hear you yelping, babe, and it wasn't from agony, I can tell you that!' There was an outraged gasp from the tall youngster, but Moira swept on. 'Not bad for your first screw, eh? Your first straight fuck, that is. The President of Leontondo – he's really a big man!' She sniggered lewdly, and there was another shocked squeak from Nicky.

'Cut it out,' I countered. 'We've all been through it. We can't help what's happening to us.'

The redhead swung towards me, her face alive with malice I never would have thought her capable of harbouring. 'And you can talk!' she jeered. 'It was easy to see you haven't had a poke from your old man in many a long month!'

Bitterly, I cursed my readiness for confessional chats in the shower room and on our mattresses in the dark, and my wounded pride made me snap back almost without thinking. 'What's wrong, Moira?' I said. 'Didn't you get enough back there to satisfy you?'

In her self-appointed prefect's role, Anita literally came between us as she stepped dripping from the shower cubicle and reached for a towel. 'Hey now,' she intervened, 'we mustn't start bitching amongst ourselves.

Things are bad enough without us falling out. We have to be there for each other, always. Right? Now, come on, please.'

'You're right,' I murmured contritely, and putting my arms up around her shoulders, I rested my forehead against her wet brow. We kissed lightly on the lips, and the next thing I knew, we were all four in a huddle, our arms around each other and kissing gently in comforting reunion. At which point the door opened and we sprang guiltily apart at the sight of the servant's leering grin.

He ushered us out of the splendid bathroom and across the long corridor into an opulent bedroom. The bed itself was a four-posted, with an elaborate canopy draped in fine muslin hangings. The silk counterpane was covered with various opened boxes, and we saw to our astonishment a variety of frothy underwear – sets of daring bras and knickers, some no more than transparent scraps of lace, in all shades and sizes.

'Dress!' the servant urged with his usual ear-splitting grin. Under his delighted gaze, we searched amongst the boxes, holding garments up to admire them before somehow choosing between them, until we had all selected some and began wriggling into the skimpy items with embarrassed titters of mirth. I had, after long consideration, chosen a pair of thong briefs. The triangle of gauze-like material just fitted over my pudenda, the string disappearing in the crack of my bottom and leaving my buttocks bare. Through the net of the light bra cups of the bra I selected could easily be seen my nipples and their surrounds, and the caress of these insubstantial scraps of clothing sent a thrilling shiver through me. There was a slender garter-belt to match, and from the generous collection offered to us, I found a pair of black nylon stockings, which I rolled slowly up my legs to clip onto the black suspenders that hung down and dissected my thighs.

Once 'dressed' in similar fashion, we stared at one another in bashful wonder. There were clearly no more clothes for us to put on over our lingerie. 'You know what?' Moira observed clinically. 'We look like a bunch of high class tarts in a brothel!' Which was exactly how we felt when the servant, whose name he told us was Joseph, showed us a selection of spike-heeled shoes, from which we made our choice. We finished dressing by slipping into lacy negligees. Tied only at the waist, they did nothing to hide our charms, and we knew that, obviously, we had not been given such finery for our own amusement, and waited with some trepidation for what was to happen next.

Eventually we were moved to yet another, smaller room this time, but it was just as luxuriously appointed as the rest of the palace, where we saw a table spread with an appetising array of cold foods, and a well-stocked bar stood in one corner manned by another white-gowned male servant. The president and his three henchmen were waiting for us, and we noted immediately the opulent silk robes they wore – with nothing underneath them, as we presently discovered. But first, we were encouraged to eat and to drink. It was a testament to our resilience, or perhaps an indication of how far along the degrading road to fatalistic acceptance we had come, that we took full advantage of the delicious spread despite our anxiety.

The excellent white wine made my head spin. I found myself answering the questions of my captors, even giggling at their bold remarks, and not even minding their playful gropes and amorous fumbling. Until they grew more determined, more intense, and the lighthearted party atmosphere evaporated as their intent became increasingly evident.

'Now for a taste of something different,' the president announced with one of his usual guffaws of exuberant mirth, and I saw, and felt, the proprietary contempt in his gaze as it moved over our scantily clad, available flesh. The four men lined up their chairs and sat back in a row, their gowns gaping open to reveal their penises, some swollen already in semi-tumescence, others limp and shrouded still and hanging coyly between their thighs.

'You...' the president's thick forefinger jabbed at me. 'I hear you're a splendid sword swallower. Come here.'

Taking a deep breath, I settled obediently on my knees between his trunk-like thighs while my companions, without further ado, took up similar positions in front of the other men. For some reason, I was strangely aware of Joseph standing by the table, and of the other silent figure posted against the wall by the bar. But, despite my self-consciousness at being watched, I meekly took the limp stump of the president's penis between my fingers. It was warm, satin-smooth, and a drop of moisture gleamed at its tip.

I gathered the rim of his foreskin between my thumb and finger and delicately slid it back, peeling free the shining head of the dome, and I shivered as I felt the throb of stirring life in my hand. I massaged it, from the thick spreading pad of his balls, up to the emergent helm, the beating increasing, the muscles pulsing until, after a few slow strokes, he was erect, hardening mightily, and the mushroom of his glans reared before me.

I lowered my face, and carefully shaped my lips to fit over that shining globe, tasting the strong flavour of his fluid, lapping it from him onto my tongue. I stretched my jaws wide, breathing heavily, and took his swelling largesse inside my mouth until he filled it, to the back of my gagging throat. I plunged forward, spearing myself on him, taking as much of him into me as I could before I choked.

The taste, the feel, the smell of him gripped me, absorbed me, so that I was no longer conscious of what was happening elsewhere. His great hands fitted round my head, his fingers wound themselves in my hair, pinning me helplessly to that rearing column. My head bobbed, I sucked and slurped and fought to breathe, until suddenly the increase of pressure and the lifting pull at my scalp told me he was about to discharge. My heart hammered in panic. When the initial surge came and his semen flooded thickly to the back of my throat, forcing me to swallow instinctively, I could not prevent my jerking away in spite of his fierce grip. I succeeded in dislodging his large erection from my lips, but knew I must make amends for what I knew was my failure. An instant later, my mouth was pressed against his still spasming penis, and I let his surging come flow thickly over my open lips and my tongue, and I even savoured its lubricious fecundity oozing thickly over my chin, dripping down my throat and onto my heaving breasts. Indeed, as the last wracking spasms went through him, I raised myself – his hands had fallen slackly away – and held his beating column tightly in my cleavage, between my breasts, and felt the final pumping fluids spill onto my perspiration-dewed skin.

'You whore,' he gasped, slumping back in his chair, but his tone was entirely of replete appreciation. His vast body heaved like a beached whale. I fell back too, off my cramped knees, and found a towel thrust onto my shoulder from behind by the hovering Joseph. I held it thankfully to my face and endeavoured to clean myself, while my exhausted gaze turned to the scene on my right, where the three submissive figures were still crouched, their heads buried between their partners' thighs. It was many minutes before the last working head was raised, and then a servant took poor Nicky, picked on again for some reason, from the room.

The men carelessly retied their gowns, and the president wagged an admonishing finger at the three of us. 'You girls,' he chortled. 'You white girls, you are all *malayas*. Prostitutes, all of you! Come, gentlemen,' he addressed his associates, 'we must punish these creatures for being so lewd.'

With that foreboding statement, he reached out and pulled me up across his broad lap. I felt the smooth warmth of his meaty thighs beneath my tummy, and to my intense embarrassment, I could also feel the clinging wetness of the tiny triangle of silk that covered my vulva. My bottom was already bare, for the string that was a part of the thong had disappeared entirely in my intimate valley, and the slender black ribbons of the suspenders hid nothing. He did not attempt to slide down the tiny knickers, but struck open-handed at the quivering pale globes exposed to him.

I wriggled and yelped, and kicked my stockinged legs in rapid little scissoring movements, which sent the high-heeled shoes flying but did nothing to deter the hefty slaps raining down on my bottom. Not that, deep down, I wanted to deter them, particularly. There could be no real resistance to whatever he chose to do to me, I knew that, and part of me found the certainty of my helplessness strangely sweet. These movements were part of the sexual manoeuvrings I knew men liked, and which, to be blushingly honest, I liked too, just as I even liked the scorching pain that spread through my rosily glowing behind, which I dimpled and clenched against his ringing slaps. His large hand was like a paddle, and the pain rose until I was squirming madly and my wet loins were grinding into his thigh.

I was close to coming, but then the burning pain took over and my yelps became ever more genuine cries of agony, until I was threshing and sobbing and begging for mercy, scalding tears meandering down my face. I was not acting now, for his pleasure or mine; the torment was real, and unbearable.

It was an agonisingly long while before he finally ceased the spanking. I hung there, blubbering, my bottom on fire. Only then did I register the similar howls of distress from the other prone girls. Panting, he flung me dismissively to the floor, where I sobbed more quietly and clutched my scorching bum for comfort. His broad face was split by a wide grin as he watched my shame and discomfort.

A little while later, we had recovered a bit, the throbbing

had subsided to a dull ache, had indeed been replaced by throbbing of another kind as we sprawled on the couches, with yet new partners in this sexual kaleidoscope we were caught up in.

I was with the other bulky representative of the president's northern tribe, laying on his lap, over which my legs were draped, my head lolling in the fleshy cushions. The flimsy bra was hanging like a scarf around my neck, and my breasts were tingling from the attention they had received from his hands and his eager lips. One of those hands was now stretching my miniscule briefs to the danger point as it delved down over my mound to the open wetness of my sex. His stubby fingers were peeling back my labia, stroking the slippery inner surfaces until my thighs writhed with the excitement coursing through me. The suspender ribbons had snapped free of the stocking tops and dangled like miniature snakes about my hips, while the nylons themselves were dragged almost to my knees in what was undoubtedly a spectacle of raunchy debauchery. However, the effect of those scrabbling fingers at my centre sent such considerations flying from my whirling thoughts. In fact, my main concern was how swiftly my amorous assailant could divest me of these few scraps of clothing, when Koloba's bellow of laughter penetrated even my excitement. There, in the centre of the room, stood a newly bathed and scarlet-faced Nicky.

At the president's enthusiastic urgings I, and the other two girls, who had been receiving equally rousing treatment, were bundled aside. Then, gathering their displaced robes about them, the men stood up and, at their leader's instigation, grabbed the weary blonde and hauled her over to the dining table. It had already been cleared of the remnants of the meal, and the luckless Nicky, her sobs only fuelling the men's desire, was spread face down on the polished surface, her arms and legs pinned out towards each corner.

She knew only too well what was to happen. The magnificent rounds of her bottom were still marked with twin red patches from her previous chastisement. They dimpled enchantingly as Koloba stood over them and lingeringly explored their texture, and let his dark fingers press deep into the inviting narrow valley between her cheeks.

'What a delectable bottom you have, my dear,' he rumbled, his voice full of warmth. 'So wonderful, so wonderful, and now we are going to warm it for you. After all, I hear tales that you are a troublesome young thing.' His bulky frame shook with mirth, and from the folds of his robe his penis rose impressively.

This time, perhaps to intensify Nicky's humiliation, he used a large salad spoon, intricately carved from smooth, richly grained olive wood, and provided by the attentive Joseph, who stood back, arms folded, to enjoy the spectacle. It made a sharp splat as it connected with her resilient flesh, and left a vivid imprint. Soon her curves were dotted with these red smudges, overlaying the marks of the earlier spanking. Her feet and hands twisted, her hips writhed and her belly ground on the hard wood. The men holding her laughed and jeered, even as they were forced to exert real effort to keep her frame stretched out and pinned down against the table. But eventually the exertion of her struggles eased, her body flinching now only at each cracking stroke, and her sobs were interspersed with mumbled pleas.

'Oh no... please... stuh-stop... I'm sorry, please!' But her anguished begging served only to prolong the torment, for it added to the pleasure the president and his cronies derived from their sport. When they did finally desist, she remained sprawled out, looking exhausted.

Koloba, body and face gleaming with sweat, flung aside his robe and, grabbing her hips, pulled her to the edge of the table so that her slender legs hung down to the floor. He parted them without ceremony, lifted her glowing buttocks and stationed himself there, driving vigorously home from behind. I stared in fascination and shameful arousal, watching those trunk-like thighs and the clenching and quivering of her paler bottom as his groin slapped against it again and again.

Until I felt my arm roughly seized and I was dragged back towards the couch I had vacated. No worries now about the wisps of clothing. They were ripped from my body with a vigour that meant they would not be fit for wearing again. My partner, the same bulky northerner who had been enjoying me before, now made me straddle him as he sat on the couch. His prick stood up like a totem pole. My heels were hooked over the gilded back of the couch as I faced him, holding him around the neck, and I lowered myself onto his straining cock. He slid easily home and I felt his pulsing length filling my narrow passage, which spasmed about the intruder with an eagerness that shocked me but about which I could do nothing. In fact, it was I who controlled the heady sensation we both experienced as I rode on his lap, and took us both on the gallop that led to our mutual breathless triumph as we raced past the winning post of fulfilment.

Chapter Nine

The sexual Olympiad continued throughout the rest of that day, and half the night that followed. To my private amazement, it was the dainty Moira who proved to be the most resilient of us all. Nicky moved through all the mechanics of the games they made us play like an automaton, except for the occasional muted groans of discomfort on account of her stinging, reddened behind. Anita and I were also too bemused by our ordeal to collect our thoughts. When we found ourselves once again herded into the bathroom, to cleanse ourselves for the next round of hectic activity, it was Moira who spoke up, her tone injecting a weird sense of normality into our far from normal situation.

'Well, that Maurice is a big bugger – and I don't just mean that fat gut of his!' I looked at her blankly. She had finished drying herself and dropped her towel. She stood with her legs slightly apart, her fingers touching her inner thighs, peeling open her labia below the rich redness of her pubic hair. She caught my look, and added, 'You know, the one that's from the same region as the president. The one with the belly; that's his name – Maurice.'

How nice, I thought sarcastically, she was on first name terms with them.

She stared at me belligerently. 'You ought to know, Jane,' she went on. 'He was shagging you after Nicky got her bum spanked again. And you were crawling halfway up the wall with pleasure.'

I felt myself blushing furiously and was glad to hide my face in the fluffy white towel.

'Well, it's no good acting coy any more, is it?' Moira pursued the subject with that air of aggression I had noted in her earlier and not much liked. 'We've all been well and truly shafted, and I suspect there's a lot more to come.'

And her prophecy proved all too accurate.

When we went back into the main room where we had shared the meal, we were passed around again, so that by the time we could see the beautifully emblazoned sunset over the dark surface of the lake through the windows, the four men had all sampled each of us. They clearly derived added pleasure from the communal nature of the couplings and, shameful though it was, I too began to sneak furtive glances about me at the permutations of male and female, dark and pale flesh, my own sexual arousal heightened by what I saw.

After an interval for more drinks and snacks, which we were urged to take our fill of, the president ordered us to lie side by side on the hastily cleared table, our hips touching, our legs dangling to the floor. We gazed up apprehensively as the four naked figures lined up facing us.

'You know me,' beamed Koloba. 'You may call me Mr President. This is Maurice,' he indicated his fellow tribesman. 'This is Samuel,' the third man was almost as tall as Koloba, his skin an equally deep shade, but he was much thinner, his facial structure angular, with a prominent jaw and large, jutting teeth of pale yellow. The fourth figure was the altogether slighter individual, with the boyish looks and skin of a lighter brown, who had been my first partner. Unlike the others, whose ebony skin was smoothly free from hair, apart from the scrub of tight curls at their bellies, he had finer whorls of hair on his chest, and also on his forearms and the front of his thighs.

'And this is David,' Koloba said, with a theatrical gesture. 'As you can see, all tribes and creeds are united under my command!' His characteristic laughter boomed out. Joseph stepped forward and handed him four eye masks of black velvet, with a thin elastic band to go round the back of the head, the kind of thing passed out on long flights to make sleep easier. We put them on as ordered, but we knew they were not intended to help us towards much needed slumber.

Sealed in darkness I lay there, every muscle tense. I could feel my hip rubbing gently against Moira's. On her other side was Anita, and then Nicky. The soles of my feet just touched the floor. My legs were almost straight, and the table's sharp edge dug into my bottom. I guessed Moira's feet must have been dangling, being that she was just that little bit shorter than me.

'Now,' the disembodied voice of the president filled the room, 'all you have to do is identify your partner. The man who will jig-a-jig you! There will be a prize if you get it right – and of course, a forfeit if you make a mistake. Right gentlemen, let the contest commence!'

I could hear laughter, whispers, and then movement. I was trembling, and my stomach muscles tensed as I waited to be penetrated. But I gasped as instead I felt the softest of fingertips stroke up my inner thighs from my knees, gently parting my legs as they did so. The pads played over the wrinkled lips of my labia and peeled them open.

The amazingly gentle fingertips slowly travelled the length of my narrow cleft, and I could feel myself moistening and blossoming beneath their attention. I nibbled my lip, and my breasts lifted in a gusty sigh. Helplessly, my buttocks clenched against the cool hardness beneath them and my hips lifted towards the increasingly invasive strokes. The fingers held me open, and even though I could not see myself, I knew they were exposing the darkening shades leading to the narrowing funnel of my vagina. It spasmed, taken over once more by its seemingly insatiable hunger, and I felt my juice flowing all the more.

My spinning brain tried to identify my seducer. Was it David? Somehow I associated such teasingly delicate foreplay with him, and I found myself hoping I would be proved right. I thought back to the bouts of sexual intercourse I had undergone during the long day. Yes, surely his fucking had been the most pleasurable? But I was no longer sure of anything except for the thunderous needs of my own flesh.

I even tried to identify the body scent, and the light fragrance of the masculine cologne he wore.

A fingertip was buried deep into the upper folds of my vulva, and had skilfully located the area around my roused clitoris, stirring me with small circular movements to which my belly and pelvis were lifting in responsive rhythm. The excitement mounted to that point where my locked muscles ached for the feel of a rampant penis driving fully home into my waiting sex – and it didn't matter whose erection it was!

My legs were lifting of their own accord, to open myself further to that compelling finger, and I closed them around a body – slick with a film of sweat. It was not David, my confused senses registered, before I felt my ankles seized in a strong grip and parted wide, so that I no longer had any contact with the body between my thighs. But then I cried out, arching upwards from the polished wood, for the wet head of an engorged and stiffened cock probed at my vulnerable flesh and nuzzled into my narrow entrance. I lifted my belly, longing only to feel the hardness enter me properly, but its owner teased me, let the slippery head slide up and down the groove of my sex, until I was wriggling madly and pleading desperately.

'Oh please, please!' I wept, my back arched and my head tossed back, all notions of pride and decency shattered by my need.

And then at last I shuddered in total ecstasy and fulfilment, as that rampant penis surged and filled me with its potency. Immediately I started to come, the waves of pleasure fanning out, sweeping over me, from my stretched and possessed cunt to the very tips of my fingers and toes. It seemed was though the very core of my flesh was bursting with star-like brilliance, dipping and soaring to an explosive climax, again and again while he plundered me. I howled blindly, the velvet blindfold soaked with my tears, and then sagged in utter exhaustion and defeat, gladly enduring the onslaught of rutting flesh until the surging release that meant the end of our union.

He left me then, drained and empty. My ankles were released, my feet dropped limply to the floor, and I lay swooning in the aftershock. Dimly, to add to my shame, I acknowledged that I had no idea who it was that had so spectacularly fucked me.

The noises to my left and right told me the others had not yet finished. But gradually the grunts and gasps and sighs eased, and quietened to easy, regular breathing.

Eventually the order came to remove the blindfolds, and wearily we eased ourselves up off the table, shamefully conscious of the hectic congress we had been put through. I blinked in the light and rubbed my eyes, and saw that the men had slipped on their silk robes. I wished we had some vestige of cover, but even the tattered scraps of our underwear had long since vanished.

'Well,' Koloba boomed, 'time for your decisions, girls. Nicky, my lovely thing, who was your partner?' She stared at him in mute, wide-eyed misery. 'Come on,' he urged jovially, 'or I'll begin to think you're teasing us so you can have that exquisite bottom of yours thrashed again.'

She gazed at him helplessly, her cheeks blushing. 'Um, I – I think it was you,' she stammered. 'Or… or perhaps…' she pointed at the grinning Maurice, and the men roared with laughter.

'Which one, girl? Come on, choose!'

Nicky looked flustered. 'Oh, er you, Mr President,' she said hastily, and he bellowed again with laughter.

'Wrong!' he cried gleefully. 'Now you, redhead! Who possessed you, my pretty little flaming-haired creature.'

Moira's fine face was lifted in an expression of defiance, and her eyes were fixed on his. 'Mr President,' she said levelly, 'I was sure I was the one you were screwing. Don't tell me I was wrong.'

He shook his head, grinning in delight. 'I cannot tell you yet,' he said. 'It would be unfair. We must not make it easy for your friends. Now, *you* guess. Who was your partner?'

The finger jabbed at me, and I stared at it. The pale curve of the short nail stood out against the solid column, and I thought of that sensitive touch arousing me so powerfully. No way! Yet I remembered, too, the fleeting contact of my legs around that corpulent and sweaty body. That was definitely not the lithe frame of David, so at a loss, I nodded at the bulky form of Maurice.

Last to guess was Anita. Her lovely head hung with shame, the black locks partly shielding her face. I watched her feet twist, the toes curl and the knees turn inward, like a little girl caught with shyness at her first school concert. One hand moved in the direction of the smiling David.

The president was aquiver with delight. 'Only my little redhead was right!' he crowed. 'I cannot disguise my prowess, eh, friends?' His companions laughed enthusiastically. 'Nicky – you had Samuel. Anita – you had Maurice.' He turned to me, his open face alive with mischief. 'And you, Jane, I give you one more chance. Guess again, little sexy mouth!'

I could not believe I could have been so mistaken, and I was even more red-faced as I turned to the slim David. But as I did, Koloba's cackles of mirth burst out with redoubled strength. 'Wrong again!' he wheezed gleefully, and his huge frame shook with laughter. I stared foolishly around me. He had taken Moira; Samuel had taken Nicky, Maurice had possessed Anita. It had to be David who had taken me. There was no one else!

Then I wished the floor would open up and swallow me, as after an interval when all of them were chortling with glee at my bewilderment, Koloba turned and beckoned the figure of the anonymous barman forward. Grinning idiotically, the fellow obeyed and lifted his white gown to his haunches, exposing a pair of sturdy legs and a thick penis that, even when dormant, hung at an impressive length between his thighs. The tears stung my eyes as I heard, as a counterpoint to the bass storm of male laughter, Moira's whispered exclamation of satisfaction.

But there was more to sting than mere tears. I had all but forgotten Koloba's words when we were first blindfolded. Now they came back all too vividly as one of the heavy couches was lugged from its position against a wall, so that it stood in the middle of the room. Nicky, Anita and I were made to stand behind it, and then to bend forward until our heads were resting in the depths of the plush red upholstery. Thus, the tight rounds of our bottoms were raised in prominent presentation for the forfeit we had to pay.

As a joke, it was a painful one. The president produced a thick strap, one end of which was split into three narrow strands. 'You see this?' he said. 'It is a tawse. Your white missionaries used it every day on us when I was at school. Apparently it was an invaluable aid to our education. I hope it serves some useful purpose for you too, my little *malayas*. Now let me introduce you.'

Cruelly, he trailed the leather thongs lightly over our bottoms, chuckling at the way our buttocks dimpled at the sinister contact. I was at one end, Nicky's toned globes filled the centre, flanked on the other side by Anita, and the stewardess was the first to receive her punishment.

There was a terrifyingly loud crack and a pitiful scream as Anita sprang upright, clawing at the fire rippling through her bottom.

'Gentlemen, some assistance here,' he chuckled, obviously savouring her distress, and immediately three figures came forward and I found my head held securely between David's knees, his hands pressing firmly down, thus trapping my upper body effectively. The hard edges of the couch's carved wooden back bit into my stomach and the tops of my thighs, but all too soon I had far greater discomfort to worry about.

With dread, I had to endure Nicky's shriek as the strap cracked across her bottom. The couch creaked with her jerked movements. I tensed, quivering with apprehension. When it came, the crack of the leather flamed like a white-hot brand over my clenched bottom. I'm sure I wailed and blubbered and squirmed and fought with my two unfortunate captors, but all I remember is the searing pain, and then the tense wait for the next explosion of leather on flesh.

And wait we did. He struck deliberately, pausing after each blow until the howling, twisting victim subsided, before moving on to the next. We were given five blows each, though the torment seemed to last a lifetime. When at last we were released we could hardly bear to straighten up. I felt as if even raising an eyebrow would add to the blaze of pain throbbing through my bottom.

It was perhaps a cruelly fitting finale to their

entertainment. Hobbling like crones, we were led out by the grinning Joseph. We flinched and winced at the kiss of the cool water under the shower, and whimpered when, as gently as we could, we bathed one another's scorched flesh. The hard red welts stood out, raised on our pale skin.

We squatted, unable to bear contact with the plastic loo seat as we relieved ourselves, too far gone in our misery to be outraged by Joseph's eager stares. We were so weary and sore with the effects of the day that we scarcely registered the luxury of the bedroom, the wide bed under whose soft clean sheets we climbed and fitted ourselves spoon-like against each other, comforted, in spite of our aches and pains, by the gentle touch of each other's bodies.

Chapter Ten

I woke from an uneasy sleep. It was still dark, and I could feel the cosy warmth of Nicky's body, the generous swell of her warm buttocks resting against my thighs, just as Anita was curled into my back. I sensed Nicky was awake too, and restless. I let my hands creep up to hold her breasts, felt their quivering movement and the hardening of her nipples against my palms. Gently my lips touched her curving shoulder, and then the fragrance of her neck.

'Come on, sweetheart,' I whispered, nibbling at her ear, and unable to help myself, I dropped my other hand down across her belly to the soft patch of pubis, stroking the curly tendrils, pressing lightly against the cushiony pad of the flesh they adorned. I quickened with excitement at the feel of the damp yielding, the upper folds of her vulva.

Her slender thighs tensed, and then her hand closed over mine and pressed it against those moist sex lips, holding it there, trapping it between her squeezing limbs.

'Everybody knows about me now,' she whispered sadly, but even as she spoke I could feel those muscles in her toned tummy and thighs moving in an instinctive welcome of my touch. 'I'm gay, aren't I? Krista knew, didn't she? I didn't even know myself.'

'Shush, darling,' I hushed, trying to comfort her. 'It's

no good – we mustn't blame ourselves. We're totally helpless here. It's not our fault.' But even as I whispered, and kissed her neck and her ear, my hand was moving, my fingers feeling the divide of her sex, which grew wet and parted to offer me freer access. And my own sex grew wetter and pulsed more imperiously as I pressed my thighs tighter to her abused bottom.

Then, just at the wrong moment, Anita turned and stirred, and I guiltily snatched my hand from the warm and moist haven between Nicky's thighs.

The greyness of dawn appeared at the window and Nicky rose, her graceful body outlined against the dim light. I joined her at the window and stared across the sloping lawns, which were covered with a thin white mist that hid the trunks of the distant trees, and above which their disembodied foliage stood out darkly. The mist cloaked the lake. We shivered in the chilly atmosphere, our naked flesh cover with goose bumps, our nipples erect.

'I wonder where Krista is,' Nicky said, her tone almost one of wistful regret.

I slipped my arm around her waist, ashamed yet acknowledging my desire to touch her. 'More to the point,' I said, noticing that only Anita was in our communal bed, 'I wonder where Moira is.'

The sun was well up, the heat of the day beginning, when Joseph reappeared to lead us to our morning ablutions. We were still soaping one another up under the soothing luxury of the warm water when the door opened and Moira came in. Her face looked pinched, there were shadows of weariness under her eyes, but she smiled at us provocatively.

Anxiously, we pressed her for details of where she had been. She stepped into the shower and we made room for her. 'The president kept me with him, all night.' She started to wash herself as she told us. 'Boy, that man is insatiable!'

'But, how come?' I asked.

'Joseph came for me when you were all asleep,' she said.

'Oh,' Nicky gasped. 'I hope they don't intend keeping us again all day today. I don't think I could stand any more.' She shuddered, and then glanced at the door and the small window. 'We ought to try to escape!' she suggested eagerly.

'Don't talk silly,' Moira scoffed. 'What on earth can we do? We haven't even any clothes.' She paused, and then pointed out, 'Don't forget, it's not just our own skin we've got to consider. Have you forgotten the others?'

Though I was fast going off Moira and her constantly confrontational attitude towards us, her supposed allies, I could not help but agree with what she said. 'She's right, Nicky,' I said gently. 'There isn't anything we can do. We just have to accept what's going on, and make sure we survive it.'

But Moira would not let it rest there. 'Let's face it, there are worse ways of fighting for survival than this,' she mused, with a mischievous twinkle in her eyes. She really did not seem overly concerned about what we were being put through.

Nicky lifted her chin and straightened herself. Somehow she rekindled a shred of her former spirit, and her blue eyes blazed. 'That might be true as far as *you're* concerned,' she said, 'but we're not all like that.'

Moira shrugged indifferently. 'Well, all I can say is that you seem to have learned mighty fast!'

Nicky looked outraged, but Moira, her damp red hair clinging to her brow, swept on with dismissive scorn. 'Listen, that's what we're here for, isn't it? To be used by anyone who fancies us? Why do you think Krista picked the four of us out in the first place? Because we're all attractive, that's why. Because we're the most shaggable of the lot. Your looks are all you've got going for you here, and you'd better believe it!'

Nicky, Anita and I silently thought about the uncompromising assessment of our worth delivered by Moira, and the brutal reality she flung at us was proved conclusively accurate within less than an hour.

We had breakfast, watched by Joseph, in the room where the sexual antics had taken place the previous evening. Our bottoms, all except Moira's, were still marked by the evidence of the tawse. We winced and shuffled as we sat, yet already learning the philosophy of living only for the moment, we enjoyed the cereal and fresh fruit, the toast and the excellent coffee, which was there for us in abundance. But then a stranger appeared in the doorway and, after taking a lingering look at our nakedness, he murmured to Joseph, who beckoned to Moira and me.

'Come!' he said simply.

Nicky sprang to my side and clung to my arm. 'Where are you going?' she blurted. 'I want to come too.'

Joseph shook his head impatiently, and with gentle haste I detached her grip. 'It'll be all right, Nicky. Just do whatever they want. We'll be back soon.' I had no idea whether that would be true as we set off down that long corridor. In spite of all my trepidation, there was still that shocking frisson of sexual thrill at the incongruity of moving unclothed in those august surroundings, of feeling the strong morning sun pouring through the rows of tall windows bathing my body in its generous warmth.

'It's his bedroom,' Moira whispered to me, and sure enough, when we entered the room indicated by the stranger, there was the figure of President Koloba, his bulk reclining on the bed in stark contrast to the refined décor around him. The bed was a circular affair, with a canopy of gathered silk above.

'Ah, my redhead,' he beamed in his usual way. 'You've brought your friend with you. That's good. You two are *good* friends, I believe?' His deep laughter rolled around the room. 'Now, show me how friendly you are. I need some entertainment, and I need some time to recover too, so for now I shall be merely a very appreciative spectator.' He wagged his finger at us, 'you naughty girls will be the death of me! But what a pleasant way to die!' He laughed; he clearly found himself very clever and amusing.

I was still staring at him in bewilderment when Moira guided me down onto the silk coverlet, so that I was almost draped across the lap of the recumbent figure, who chortled appreciatively again. I felt Moira's slim frame pressing intimately against me; breast to breast, belly to belly, her thighs entwining with mine. And then before I could resist she kissed me, and I admit I felt my passions stir at the feel of her energetic little tongue. My spinning mind had time only to register that I must not struggle, except perhaps to emulate and return her embraces.

My rebelliously naughty body was all too willing to play the part assigned to it. We writhed and twisted, glued together on the rumpled silk, avidly seeking contact with each other, our hands and fingers clawing, searching, over every soft plane and curve, moving swiftly down to our rapidly moistening sex lips which opened greedily for more attention.

I could feel Moira's fingers buried deep in the clinging sheath of my vagina, while my own squelched in her receptive tightness. But who would have succumbed first to their desire was never ascertained, for to our feverish dismay, the president tired of his role as spectator. He prised us apart, his hands firmly clasped in our hair, and then without letting go, he dragged our heads down to the expanse of his lower belly, where his penis thrust up in urgent need of our mutual attention.

So we found ourselves crouching, either side of those substantial thighs, fingers working and our lips and tongues nibbling at the dark column of his erection and its large helmet. Our flushed cheeks bumped, and our moist lips touched around the veined stalk. The dome was coated with the clear fluid that was seeping from the aperture at its crest.

Then without warning he rolled us away, I felt my ankles seized, I was pinned back on my shoulders and my captured feet were folded over them, so that I was mercilessly exposed, my sex lifted to his avid view. He knelt, his knees resting against my buttocks, and drove his rearing prick straight at my exposed sex. I felt him prod and slide easily between my gaping labia to the inner tightness that welcomed his piston-like lunge. He ploughed into me and my back curved as I rocked in time to his thrusts, and soon, to my shame, I shook in the ferocity of a breathtaking orgasm, until I felt the potent flood of his own climax filling and fulfilling me, and I slumped like a rag doll beneath his immense weight in limp exhaustion.

He sank back on the pillows and waved us wanly away, in the direction of an adjoining door. It led to a bathroom that was unbelievable. The fittings were all in midnight blue, the taps and showerheads in gold. The lavatory and bidet pedestals stood side-by-side, and double washbasins snuggled in equally cosy intimacy. There was a tiled shower area large enough for two people behind the glass screens. But pride of place was taken by the splendid circular sunken bath. Surrounding it was a wide shelf covered with a host of fragrances – soaps, oils, and foams, in exotic glass jars.

The bath was full and steaming fragrantly, the surface covered with silky white bubbles, so we took it as an invitation and slipped into its soothing luxury, gratefully sinking down until we were submerged to our shoulders.

Part Two – Moira's Story

Chapter Eleven

'Oh, no... please don't stop!' My head threshed on the pillow and my fingers clutched at the dark head which was devouring me, that lapping, sucking mouth eating at the very heart of me, drawing out every morsel of sexual desire from my spasming body, spread and aching on its rack of physical pleasure, until I could stand no more. I cried out at the engulfing rush of an orgasm, felt it sweep irresistibly through me, sending even my brain into whirling fragments with its elemental force.

When I came to I was shivering, crying, my fingers now relaxed in the tangled hair. I could feel Jane's face on my inner thigh, her breath cool and tickling my pubes and skin. The drops of perspiration, and her own tears, mingled with the flood of love juice she had drawn from me, and which glistened liberally on her face and my tummy.

'Oh, I loved that,' I sighed, and meant it too, as I gently tried to lift her face from between my thighs. At last she moved until our warm bodies snuggled together, her breasts against mine, and I kissed her lips, shivering in post-orgasmic thrill at the tangy flavour of my sex.

The last three days had been like heaven, so unexpected

after all the trauma we had been put through. After the scene in that fabulous bath, and Koloba had screwed me in it, literally under Jane's nose, he had taken himself off and Jane and I were left wondering, like we did most of the time, what would happen next.

No one came near us – not Koloba, and none of his cronies like fat Maurice or Samuel or David. And still no Krista. If only we had known, we could have enjoyed ourselves even more, but we did pretty well anyway, following our newly learned philosophy of sufficient unto the minute...

Though President Koloba had forced our hand, so to speak, I knew really that Jane fancied me just as much as I did her. Up until then things were getting a bit fraught between us and the other two girls, but we were bound to be tense, given the circumstances.

I believe she was telling the truth when she said she had never had bi-sexual tendencies, until Krista had initiated her in the dark under the plane – of all places! That was the great thing about our interlude at Koloba's palace – that was when we really got to know each other, because, in between all the sex, we lay for hours, talking and talking. We laid ourselves bare – mind as well as body – and it was as wonderful as all the lovemaking sharing all these intimacies with each other. Ironically enough, our sexual imprisonment gave us all the chance to be more honest and open than we had ever been with anyone before. At least that's how I felt and I'm pretty sure it was the same for Jane.

Once we let ourselves go, it all hung out, as they say. I'm sure Nicky and Anita were shocked, in spite of all the things the four of us had been put through. Even Jane found it hard going at first. She blushed like mad when I came out and said what I felt. 'I didn't need Koloba to force me to make love with you, Jane.' I told her. 'I've been up for it ever since I saw you.' And it was true, and she knew it. And she felt the same way, as we proved over and over during that very enjoyable three days.

The other two girls left us to get on with it. To be honest, I was hoping they would get it together too. Nicky was ripe for it, but she didn't know if she was coming or going since the hijack. First of all, she had been singled out by Krista, who had broken her in to lesbian loving, literally, it seemed. And then, when she was still reeling from that, she had found herself being shafted by four men, the president and his mates. It had certainly been hard for her to take, in more ways than one. By then she would have been glad enough to crawl between Anita's thighs for a little comforting, but unfortunately Anita was too straight to let anything like that happen out of choice. Still, whether they approved or not, Jane and I were stuck to each other like glue by the first of our three stolen nights and days of bliss – and we stayed that way as often as we could.

It was more than great. It took me back to those giddy days when I first met Jack. I tried to share the magic of the memory with Jane, my latest lover. From my adolescent schooldays, I knew I had a strong bi-sexual element in my make-up. I wanted to be with girls, I had crushes on them, and I avoided boys as a dangerous, uncouth species. Yet there was nothing butch about me. I was ultra feminine, the most girlie of girlies, with my ruby ringlets and dainty skirts and my frilly bits underneath. I was all too breathlessly willing to be the submissive one. Not that I went for the butch types. I like a girl to look like a girl. But I liked her to be bossy, too!

It was not Jack at all I fancied when I first met him. I was seventeen and head over heels with his beautiful blonde cousin, Katy, who was a year older than me, and a lot more worldly-wise. I was a virgin. Not with girls, but no prick had passed, or got anywhere near, the dewy portals of my pussy. Whereas for the delectable Katy I was prepared to surrender everything.

She was certainly dominant enough for my taste. Physically, she could be quite rough. Not only in her love play, though that, too, left its mark in the love bites I had to strive to disguise on my throat.

We were on a family holiday, guests of her folks in their rambling Victorian house on the North Yorkshire coast, when she brought to light the masochistic facet of my sexuality, which responded to the rough stuff – the kneeling astride me, the pinning of my arms above my head as I started to come noisily in the excess of my emotion.

Then one day, up in her room, when the family was out but we were too scared to undress and climb under the sheets in case anyone came and caught us in the act, we were fooling around when she pulled me over her knee and scooped up my skirt over my behind. My bum was hardly hidden; I was wearing a pair of skimpy white panties, with a thin blue piping of lace and two tiny embroidered forget-me-nots on the small triangle of the front panel. Most of my bottom was on show, as the tiny panties had ridden deep into the crack. Even so, as I lay there I felt Katy's nails scratch lightly at my skin as she slipped her fingers into the elastic and slowly eased the panties down off my bottom.

I was as highly aroused as she was, and I could feel my thighs and tummy rubbing against the rough material of her jeans. I thought she was going to slip my panties down and off my legs, but she left them just clear of my dimpling bottom, stretched across the backs of my thighs. Then her hand was exploring those clenching curves, her fingers gently tracing the deep cleft itself, before, with a sudden sting whose hot burn made me yelp, she began to spank me. Lightly and deliberately at first, so that I felt each ringing slap and savoured its warmth spreading through my buttocks, to mingle with and add to the melting heat I could feel a few vital inches away, in that other moistening area which was the centre of my excitement.

Then she slapped harder and quicker and my struggles grew more genuine. Still I hung helplessly over her knee, and still I grew wetter and more aroused. My hips began to squirm. My bottom was burning quite painfully, and my yelps became interspersed with genuine tears. But the desire grew remorselessly, in unison with the glowing pain of my throbbing bottom. So that when, panting triumphantly, she rolled me off her knee to watch me grovelling, panties at half-mast and hands clawing at my stinging behind, despite my scalding tears I was afire with sexual hunger. Seconds later she was kneeling over me, her fingers dipping into my wet sex, and seconds after that I stiffened, sobbing against the force of the climax tearing through me.

I did not believe her when, hiding on the slope of our favourite sand dune one blustery afternoon, kissing and cuddling, she insisted I should not be exclusively gay. 'There's an awful lot of pleasure to be had from a man,' she assured me, with a cheeky grin. I gazed back in wounded reproach, but she laughed unrepentantly. 'Don't look like that, my pet. Believe me, you'll feel differently once you've tried it.'

And that was when she first mentioned Jack, her cousin – and, she hinted broadly, her lover, though she tormented me by never actually admitting that she had gone the whole hog and screwed him. I stared, feeling betrayed, the tears glistening large in my tragic eyes. 'He's coming up at the weekend,' she went on, seemingly oblivious to my jealousy. 'He's drop-dead gorgeous, and I know you'll wet your pretty little knickers after just one look at him.'

Well, as it happens, Katy was not far wide of the mark. Except that my excitement was caused more by the abstract obsession with what it would be like to have a rigid cock, any cock, burrowing into me than with the desire that it should be Jack's cock that would have the honour of being first past the post, as it were. Not that he wasn't handsome, just as she had said; he certainly was attractive, though not in an obvious way. In fact, truth to tell, it was Jack's resemblance to Katy, in his fine features and slender boyish grace, which drew me to him in the first place.

To begin with, I was more jealous of his obvious intimate relationship with his cousin, but I quickly realised they were both playing up to me for all they were worth. Their delight with their success sickened me further, but there was nothing I could do about it. I even noted the masochistic element in me, which extracted a perverse pleasure from the very misery their behaviour caused me. They were aware of this too. Initially, I thought only Katy knew me well enough to understand this quirk in my nature, but I soon discovered just how close the fiendish pair were in their thoughts as well as their looks.

Things came to a head one wet afternoon when a thunderous deluge, which only the peak August holiday can produce, kept us trapped indoors in the Victorian seaside house owned by Katy's parents. My folks and hers were downstairs somewhere in one of the corniced living rooms off the long hall. Which made what Jack and Katy planned and did all the more shocking, even though we three were hidden away in the sloping attics, where the red knuckled skivvies had slept exhaustedly when the house was new.

Everything between we three was all hints and giggles, nothing defined or clear-cut, so I was embarrassed as hell when Katy grabbed me and began feeling me, pulling me to her and kissing me in a way that was far from the innocent chums' fashion which I still thought Jack might assume existed between us.

'She's a randy little sod underneath all this prissy exterior,' Katy told him mockingly. 'Give me a hand and I'll show you what I mean.' Even then I was sure she was just mucking about, that she would stop before things got out of hand.

But I was wrong.

Suddenly they were both pinning me down, and Jack was lying across me heavily enough for me to feel my breasts squashed flat against his chest, while he bent my arms up over my head and held my wrists in a painful grip. His grinning face loomed over me, so that I could not see what Katy was up to. But I could feel all right, as her fingers plucked at my belt, and then unzipped the fly of my jeans and began to drag them down over my wriggling hips. I let out a shriek, and felt the cool air on my belly and thighs, the tightly clinging material like binding just above my knees.

'Shut her up,' she giggled, hauling them further down. 'She'll have everybody up here, complaining like that.' Next thing I knew Jack's face swooped closer and his mouth was fastened over my parted lips, while his tongue plunged invasively to the back of my throat. My struggle ceased with magical abruptness, as if he had sucked all resistance from me. I could feel the strength ebbing away from my watery muscles, the flowing weakness spreading from my tummy, fanning outwards from that moist junction which was hidden by the black silk triangle of my knickers, against which my mound seemed to swell with newly released urgency. As if he knew exactly what was happening within me, he released my mouth and eased his weight from my breast. His fingers plucked unhurriedly at the buttons of my shirt, undoing them, so that it fell open revealing my black bra, from which my breasts rose in an effort to gather air into my straining lungs.

They stripped me with teasing deliberation. Katy removed my trainers and socks before she tugged the jeans clear of my feet. Jack lifted my arms and shoulders from the old mattress upon which they had laid me, to get my shirt off. I lay shivering in my bra and panties, making no effort to prevent them.

They knelt over me, and their eyes met. They nodded mischievously. His fingers were busy at my back, with a wicked skill I had never associated with a boy only a year or so older than me. He unhooked the bra clip, eased down the shoulder straps and peeled the cups from my breasts, and his eyes devoured me.

I gasped as I felt Katy's fingers at my hips, and then the elastic of my panties being eased down to peel away my last concealment.

Without pretence now they assaulted me with rough love-play, but the attack only heightened the fever of my excitement. I spasmed, close to an orgasm, as Jack's mouth settled over one nipple while Katy's tongue lapped at the other. Her fingers teased and plucked my labia, parting the wet tissue, which flowered, engorged and throbbing with hunger to feel her penetrate me.

I was sobbing, shaking uncontrollably, sure that any second now I should feel for the first time a penis plunge deep into my tightness. So it made the shock all the more brutal when, trapped in that world of helpless need, I suddenly found myself plucked upright, thrust onto a rickety wooden chair to which I was tied by wrists and ankles, with enough force to make my struggles to escape utterly useless. Katy then produced a roll of broad green parcel tape, with which she gagged my protesting mouth until I was unable to make any sound other than a feeble, muffled, outraged, 'M-m-mumph!'

'Right, my little virgin, look and learn,' she said, and with all the aplomb of practised strippers, she and Jack undressed in front of me. I had little choice but to follow her advice, and there was the penis I had thought was going to fuck me, in all its rigid glory. I watched its stiffness disappear into the mouth of a transformed Katy, who knelt submissively at his feet and sucked him until he was forced to seize her blonde hair and pull her away. His prick gleamed with her saliva, and his own juices that seeped from the tiny slit at the dark helm. Which disappeared yet again as he grabbed her thighs and upended her on the mattress. Her feet were lifted and pointed directly towards me. He plunged between them and I watched, entranced, the powerful rise and fall of his bottom, the tempo quickening to the last frantic, rutting ride home, the cheeks dimpling as he fucked her to perfection. The upturned feet jerked in their mad dance of release, and at that very instant my thighs tightened and my stomach knotted in their own crescendo as I came in a shattering flood, which made the chair wobble and creak on the dusty floorboards.

Chapter Twelve

Jane and I moved to the floor of the luxurious bedroom for more intimacy. We made a nest of the plentiful blankets and pillows, and left the large bed to Nicky and Anita. They could not see us – unless they made a point of looking – but no doubt they could hear every sob and sigh as we brought each other to summits of ultimate bliss. It was as well that they weren't able to overhear our whispered confessions while we lay entangled in sated contentment – if they had, they might have been further shocked.

Jane finally told me of the sexual problems she was facing inside her marriage. How Carl, a whiz kid in his career as a trade consultant for some mega international company, was far from hot under the sheets. 'At least he isn't with me,' she brooded, but I gathered her suspicions that he might be getting his oats off elsewhere were not really serious. 'We hardly seem to touch each other any more. I know he's got his career and everything, but it's like he's gone off me altogether. I just don't understand. We love each other, we really do. But then sex and love... how much do they really have to do with each other?' she mused out loud.

I was very intrigued. 'How do you cope?' I asked her. 'I mean, what do you do to get your fun if you don't fuck? I gather *you* haven't gone off sex too. And don't tell me you have because I won't believe you.'

She gave a self-reproaching tut. 'I learnt to become quite efficient at DIY,' she admitted with obvious difficulty, 'and I have to admit I strayed a little bit, too. Not much, but I confess, I had one or two sneaky little affairs.'

My mind returned to my own relationship with Jack. Maybe it was the kinky nature of its beginnings that gave it the necessary sparkle and fascination that, for me, it had never lost. Vividly, I recalled that first hectic passion yet again, when he and Katy had forced upon me the role of voyeur. I pictured myself sitting there, my arms and ankles abraded at the strength with which I twisted and fought against the bonds that held me to that wooden chair. I would never forget the helplessness that served to fan the heat of my sexual excitement as I watched their beautiful, undulating bodies, until my own wayward flesh found its release. Wickedly, they continued to keep me simmering with frustration, until after a few days I was practically begging Jack to put me out of my virgin misery and screw me. And it was not just Jack I begged – all pride was forgotten as I blubbered and pleaded with Katy to allow me the privilege of surrendering my body to that rearing, all-important penis.

It was quite a come down, but it was worth it when, at last, after more teasing on that musty mattress that left me literally running with need, I felt for the first time Jack's penis plough into my lubricated, eager pussy, and seconds later send me spasming in an explosive climax which was infinitely more wonderful than my wildest, rudest dreams had prepared me for.

But for the moment, the situation Jane and I found ourselves in contained more than enough excitement and fear even for me. She and I both knew that the idyll we were sharing could not last. After our third night in the unaccustomed splendour of the palace, we were woken at first light by a crisply dressed Krista, who stood over us with a smile on her lovely face that made our hearts pound with alarm. I could feel the colour sweep up from my breasts to my cheeks as she stared knowingly at Jane and me.

A little earlier, when we had for the moment exhausted our appetite for each other, we climbed into the soft warmth of the big bed, where Anita and Nicky were sleeping in chummy but chaste harmony. But the cool grey eyes of our captor seemed to penetrate to our very thoughts, so that I was convinced she was aware of every detail of our new intimacy. The instinctive way in which I snuggled into Jane's arms no doubt served to confirm what she already knew or suspected.

'Well, my little whores,' that throaty voice proclaimed, 'how have you all been without me?' She reached out and playfully ruffled Nicky's hair, which could not now be described as 'cropped', as it was when I first saw her. I thought how thoroughly we had all been broken into our submissive role, for the athletic girl did nothing except bow her head now and blush a fiery scarlet, which drew a further chuckle from Krista; a chuckle which set me on edge, for beneath its lightness I could detect a hint of jealousy.

But she kept up this act of light-hearted casualness all the way through a leisurely breakfast, served to us by Joseph. As usual, we were completely naked. I felt myself blushing, ridiculously coy when Krista's eyes examined us, as though she had never observed us naked before. It seemed a lot longer than five days since we had seen her.

'I have missed you, my little whores,' she said, grinning. 'Though I know you never gave me a thought, what with all those men you have had to entertain, and do not worry, I have been hearing all about you. But your fun is over,' she went on menacingly. 'You are well and truly back with me now. Well,' she qualified, with a sinister chuckle, 'two of you are.' And she crooked a finger at Jane and me. 'You two, come with me.'

With a last anxious glance at the other two frightened faces, we rose and followed her out of the room.

Once again reminded of our nudity, which seemed designed to strip us of our sense of uniqueness, of our individuality, we padded in her wake along the corridor with its closed doors and heavily framed portraits of forgotten colonial administrators hanging on the walls. She led us to a narrow staircase and down to the ground floor, somewhere at the rear of the building near the kitchens. We could hear chattering voices and laughter, and the sound of clattering dishes and running water.

Then we felt the full heat of the sun on our shoulders, and the pinprick of gravel beneath our feet. A few yards from the door was a Land Rover, possibly the same one as before, and at Krista's curt order we climbed over the tailgate. She joined us in the back.

The low bench seats were hard beneath our bottoms and we shifted uncomfortably, our knees bumping, during a ride that lasted too long, the road growing progressively worse until we were being flung and jarred about, so that it was a great relief when at last we reached journey's end.

A quick glance around as we alighted showed us that we were in a fenced compound of a much more modest building than the one we had just left. It was a single storey edifice, with a steep roof of red corrugated iron, and the rendered walls were painted an ugly yellow. There was a wooden veranda that ran around the building, with a low wooden railing at its outer edge. The windows were small, and on the inside of the glass, they were lined with grilles of stout metal mesh. Two guards lounged at the front door, and we could see two other guards at the gate of the compound. The grinning soldiers stared lecherously at us, and then we were inside, in a sparsely furnished room, the polished concrete floor, scattered with a few rush mats, cool beneath our bare feet.

To our surprise, Krista's three original accomplices came in through an adjoining door. It had been three months since we had last seen them, but theirs were not faces we were likely to forget easily. Two of them stared at us with undisguised lust, which made me wonder how Krista had managed to keep us out of their sight and out of their hands for so long, while the leader eyed us with a cooler regard, befitting his status as their superior, I suppose. Nevertheless, his gaze covered us with lingering appreciation.

'Welcome, ladies.' He smiled, treating us to the full effect of his handsome face. In spite of myself, I felt a stupid adolescent blush rising from my throat, and I quickly stared down at my toes. 'I hope you like your new home,' he went on in a pleasant voice. 'Not quite up to the elegance of President Koloba's residence, but I am sure you will get used to it, in time. As you will have gathered by now, it is conveniently out of the way and extremely secure.'

Jane cleared her throat and spoke in an appeasing tone. 'Please, can you tell us if – when we'll be going home? Has anything—!' she gave a cry of alarm as Krista stepped forward and grabbed her by the hair, twisting her arm up behind her back, and forced her down to her knees.

'You can see they've missed me, can't you?' Krista smiled, keeping Jane's wrist trapped spitefully high between her shoulder blades. Jane's head was down, and she was whimpering quietly. 'Who gave you permission to speak?' Krista barked, and briefly increased the pressure on Jane's arm until the girl let out another shrill yelp of agony.

'No one!' Jane managed to mutter miserably. 'I'm suh – sorry!'

Krista flung her away and she fell sprawling, clutching at her upper arm. She lay there on her front, cowering, making no effort to rise.

'I can see I'll have to lick you two into shape,' Krista commented, chuckling, 'and there's no time like the present, as they say. Is everything ready?' She nodded towards the inner door.

The shorter and more thickset of the men nodded and grinned expressively. 'All is as you wish,' he said, leering at us, and my heart quickened with fear. But he then looked extremely disappointed as the leader spoke, with crisp impatience.

'No, we must go,' he said. 'We will be back tonight. Have fun – there are guards in plenty should you need any help.' He glanced at Krista, but the blonde head shook firmly.

'No, I can handle things,' she said confidently. 'Do not worry.' She prodded Jane's hip with her boot. 'Come, whores, I have a wonderful surprise for you.'

Intrigued as well as frightened, we followed her as she led us through the doorway into a short corridor. We passed a bathroom and a shower room, and I guessed that the door opposite led to bedrooms. Then we entered a spacious room at the far end of the bungalow, which certainly was a bedroom.

A large bed filled the centre of the space, but there was little other furniture except a few cane chairs placed against one wall. But what caught our gaze, and occupied our full attention, was the bizarre spectacle on the bed itself. Side by side, chained and manacled by wrists and ankles to the head and foot rails, lay two sleekly gleaming black figures. The black, however, was not the colour of their skin, but the tight suits that covered them from head to toe. It was made of a stretchy smooth material, and literally did conceal every inch of them, except for a tiny vent at their nostrils, and a slightly larger slit that outlined the shape of their mouths. There was one other opening in these weird garments, and it was this fact which chiefly drew our astonished gaze, for sprouting from their groins through an aperture designed expressly for the purpose were their penises, both of a delicate brown hue, one a little darker than the other, that proclaimed the two men to be Caucasian.

But there were differences between them; for example, the penis on the right as we faced them was much the larger. Even dormant it was nearly twice the length of its more normal-sized counterpart. It draped heavily across the fold of thigh, the helm still shrouded in its puckered hood of foreskin. By contrast, the other penis looked as though it was standing up a little, in a kind of semi-erection. The purple dome of its glistening helm was uncovered, yet the brown, concertinaed column poking from the hole in the black suit was only a little longer than the helm itself. The whole squat appendage, from tip to base, was a generous few inches, and yet it seemed an unimpressive length compared to the other penis. It was not actually in any state of erection, and yet it appeared to be standing proud from the supine body.

Both these weird figures looked like some strange sci-fi cartoon creation. They were both slim, and the one with the smaller penis was quite a bit shorter than the fellow by his side. We could see the shape of their torsos, the upward thrust of their ribcages and the hollowed sweep of flat stomachs. But the sleek roundness of the eyeless skulls and those clinging black bodysuits, though showing every dip and curve and projection, gave us absolutely no idea of what they looked like. And the only part of them on view, those sprouting penises, added only to the strange sense of disembodiment.

'Right, my dear girls, you can see what miserable specimens of so-called manhood we have here,' Krista sneered. 'Let us see if you can bring these limp worms to life.'

She directed me towards the fellow with the smaller prick, while Jane knelt astride the legs of the other guy, whose tool was already stirring and lifted tremulously from his thigh even before she touched him. Krista had acquired a whip, of slender triple leather strands. We needed no such encouragement to bend, literally, to our task, though we both felt its biting lash across our backs and our lifted buttocks as we reached forward and got on with our bizarre task of arousing two anonymous flack figures.

My man's cock looked like one of those mysterious toadstool fungi you see growing in the woods. I took it gently between thumb and forefinger, shook it, and let my fingers stroke down the few inches or so of warm column below that shiny dome. I felt a responsive beat. There was an emission of clear fluid. I lapped gingerly, taking in its tangy, acrid flavour. The juice flowed freely, but despite the increasing vigour of my strokes, the thing scarcely grew in length at all, and although there was a certain residual firmness about the shaft, it gave no real indication of stiffening into the rigidity of a proper erection. I could hear Jane sucking to my right, and had a sense of her dark head bobbing diligently. In desperation, I kissed the helmet between my fingers, and then took it inside my mouth, sucking hard, and sliding my lips down until I had him completely inside.

At last! I felt him swell and press against the roof of my mouth, while his thigh muscles locked. They rubbed against my breasts, and his groin lifted slightly to meet my caresses. Then, with a shudder that I felt pass through me, he ejaculated with startling suddenness and without warning straight into my working mouth. His thick seed flooded me and I choked, pulling my mouth away even as I instinctively swallowed his sperm, and then I howled at the flare of agony across my buttocks as Krista cut me with the whip.

'Finish it!' she urged hoarsely, and obediently I covered his cock again with my mouth and lapped up the residue of his come until I had swallowed it all.

Gasping, I turned my head and saw Jane's crimson face working furiously at the column that rose splendidly upright. The helm gleamed, and the rigid shaft was roped with twisted veins, throbbing with the urgency of its desire. Then, with a swift and brutal efficiency, Krista hauled Jane off the captive figure and flung her carelessly to the floor, where she lay, staring in appalled fascination, just as I did, at the most bizarre spectacle of all in that weird episode.

The German girl had stripped off her clothing below the waist. With her shirt hanging loose, she straddled her victim, seized that thick column in her fist and guided it to her cunt, which descended and impaled itself upon that erect weapon until it had disappeared entirely inside her. She rode him furiously, her transformed face aflame with passion, humping down on the black form in a frenzy of sexual hunger, and it wasn't long before she gave a great cry of fulfilment. She ground herself in a last violent spasm against him while the convulsive shudders of a climax tore through her, and then she groaned and toppled sideways onto the bed, dragging herself clear, exposing again that still impressive penis, whose length gleamed now with the coating of their combined fluids.

Chapter Thirteen

We were frozen into immobility while Krista sat slumped on the edge of the bed, her bent shoulders heaving. I could hear the laboured breathing of the two chained men, the only sound in the room, until Krista dragged herself to her feet, swore vituperatively in German, scooped up her discarded clothing, and stormed out without a glance in our direction. Jane slowly picked herself up from the floor, and almost absently, our fingers traced the stinging weals dissecting our buttocks and the backs of our thighs. We gazed at each other in mute shock and consternation, glancing at the open door, and then at the two trussed figures on the bed.

My mind was racing in overdrive, and Jane's thoughts were close behind. These men were clearly prisoners, like us, so it didn't need any great leap of imagination to deduce that they must be hostages from the plane the same as us. And from this conclusion came the next bizarre thought.

'Jack?' I whispered, appalled. Surely that modest specimen of a male penis could not belong to my husband? I was overwhelmed with the awful realisation that, very possibly, I could not even recognise my own husband's penis.

'Jack?' I repeated, a little more loudly. 'Are you… is that you…?' At my words, the taller figure began to struggle, so that the short chains securing him to the bed rattled and clinked. But I still could not be sure it was him. Was this writhing his way of confirming my suspicions? I bent close, and realised from the muffled noises coming from behind that faceless mask that he was very effectively gagged.

Meanwhile, Jane had approached the other, smaller figure. She glanced over at me, her eyes large, the tears spilling from them, and I knew at once that she had recognised her husband. Well, I thought with unfair sarcasm, if Jack had a dick like *that* I would know him too.

Her soft voice was tentative as she whispered his name, but she knew it was all right, I could tell. She laid a hand on his thigh. 'Carl, are you all right?' she asked. 'I daren't do anything. Krista will be back in a minute. Just lie still for a while longer.'

A convulsive shudder passed through his frame and he began to snuffle, his chest rising and falling violently in what was clearly a fit of weeping. Jane looked at me again, her own tears falling plentifully, in an agony of appeal, but just then Krista returned, once more dressed immaculately, though her cheeks showed telltale spots of colour which owed nothing to make-up.

'Well, girls, have you got to know our guests yet?' she mocked. 'I think maybe you have an idea, yes? Why do you not find out for sure? You will see there are fastenings at the back of the neck. Go on, you have my permission, and I am sure they will be relieved to be out of those things. They must be sweating like the pigs they are.

'But no,' she stopped us abruptly as we moved to obey

her at once, 'keep to your partners, yes? The ones you are already so well acquainted with.'

Cruelly, she made us swap, so that I was dealing with the slender figure I had sucked to completion, while Jane dealt with the other – the one she had aroused, the one Krista had fucked, the one I suspected was my Jack.

The hoods were the first to come off. They were attached around the neck by a zip fastener, and we had to peel them off the gasping victims, not without difficulty.

But the flushed and sweating face I revealed came as a great shock to me. I had anticipated the green tape wadded firmly over his lips, but what shocked me so much that I gasped aloud was the white, shaven skull.

I glanced across and saw, with another shock even though I had prepared myself for it, the features of my husband Jack, who amazingly managed a smile and a wink when our eyes met for the first time in three eventful months. I instinctively leaned towards him, but there was a singing hiss behind me and a ripple of fire kissed my back and shoulders as Krista lashed me. I pulled back and returned to my task, sobbing as I did so, which was to continue stripping the clinging costume from the slim body of Jane's husband, Carl.

To get the suits off them Krista had to unlock the chains, and then a further surprise awaited us, for as I peeled away the soaking garment I saw that the whole of Carl's body had been totally shaved of hair so that his skin was as smooth as alabaster.

Another swift glance across at Jack reassured me he had not been subjected to a similar indignity. His hair, unkempt and lank with sweat, was thankfully still adorning his head, and all his body hair seemed to have remained untouched.

The two men eased themselves stiffly into a sitting position, and massaged the red circlets of chafed flesh at their wrists and ankles that betokened their hours of bondage. I noted almost despairingly that neither Jack nor Carl showed any signs of resistance. They did not even remove the gagging tape from their mouths. That was left for us to do, upon Krista's nod of permission, of course.

'There now, how sweet,' she mocked. All four of us were now huddled close on the bed, yet we were afraid to embrace in case we should incur her displeasure. 'I will leave you to get reacquainted. This will be your new home.' She waved towards the door. 'You have freedom here, and there is a boy who will do the cooking and the cleaning. You will be safe here, but just one thing to remember; there are guards all round the place, so any attempt to escape and you will be shot on the spot. Understand?' And then, with a final patronising wag of her finger, she left us, and we sat without moving or speaking until we heard her voice outside, the slam of a vehicle door, and its engine's departing roar.

The history of what had happened to the men after we were segregated was learned piece by piece, gradually, over many conversations and reflections in the days that followed our reunion. To our amazement, those days extended into weeks, and then months.

At first, the men had been treated rather better than we were. They were not humiliated as we had been. Not in general, that is, but there had been exceptions. It was, as I have said, over many days and nights of whispered confessions that the picture of these events emerged. Tearfully compelled by her own need for the catharsis of sharing her secret, Jane told me one night how Carl had been picked out by one of the hijackers, and forced to perform fellatio on him. As she sobbed out her tortured tale, I could visualise all too clearly the whirl of conflicting emotions surging through Carl's reeling mind as he knelt there sucking another man. He claimed, when he confessed to Jane what had happened to him, that it was the first time he had performed such an act, and for all I know he may have been telling the truth. But if it was so, I am sure it was merely the realisation of many such secretly fantasised scenarios from adolescence onwards – exactly as Jane's encounter with Krista beneath the nose of the plane had been for her. Disturbed he might have been, but thrilled he certainly was, I would bet my life on it. My first study of Carl's slender, naked frame, his delicate good looks, and his not bad, but also not very impressive penis, convinced me that this was one confused guy, whether he was prepared to admit it or not.

By the time we came together at the bungalow, his relationship with the hijacker was no secret any more. Jack told me how quickly it had become common knowledge that Carl was servicing his male captor. And it wasn't just blowjobs he was delivering, either. There were times when Carl would come hobbling back, his backside covered in the weals and bruises that indicated the sadistic pleasure his captor was taking in beating him.

As I said, it was a long time before the full picture came

out, including the shameful body-shave the loathsome hijacker, in front of several of his cronies, had inflicted upon his chosen victim. And yet the truth is that in those first heady hours of being reunited, I was far too preoccupied with Jack to have any thoughts, one way or the other, about Carl.

Chapter Fourteen

When Krista returned some days later she was with Khotan, the one who had clearly been the leader of the initial hijack. For the next few days they spent the nights at the compound, but they were away during daylight hours.

And then one morning the houseboy called us for breakfast at the civilised hour of eight o'clock. We all six took breakfast around the dining table, with the houseboy serving the simple but substantial meal. We were all somewhat flustered by Khotan's presence with Krista, and the sinister fact that we still had no real idea of who they were, or what they wanted from us, added to our unease.

Khotan was an unknown quantity – and a very dangerous unknown quantity, that much was for certain.

He chatted easily enough, and had an urbane manner that made me even more aware of my nakedness. Yet his features gave away nothing of his real thoughts, even when the dark eyes passed over the unavoidable fact of our nudity, and we did not initiate conversation, but waited to be addressed and answered only direct questions with direct answers.

So when he casually announced that we were the only hostages left, that the others had all been safely released and gone home, we stiffened with shock and dread, unable to respond, and waited tensely for further enlightenment.

'So we have more time to devote to you,' Krista said, smiling – a smile that made my flesh crawl. But her next words were addressed to a mortified Jane only. 'And you in particular,' she said. 'I have neglected you so much lately, yes? You poor darling.' She glanced pointedly at Carl's pale form, and in particular at his dormant penis. 'I dare say you have been missing our fun together,' she sneered at her, 'with nothing to replace me.' She laughed and turned her gaze on me. 'Especially since dear Moira here has been too busy with her man to bother with you the way she used to.'

She got up, moved round the table and tousled Jane's hair. 'Come with me now, and I will make it up to you. I have an hour or so free. Excuse us, won't you?' She smiled round at us, and then without another word she guided the scarlet-faced Jane up from her chair, and led her out of the room.

The three of us who were left avoided one another's gaze in an agony of embarrassment. Then Khotan gave a quiet chuckle, and I flinched as he reached out and laid his hand casually over my wrist. 'In turn, I must ask you to excuse me also, gentlemen,' he stated. 'I will see you later.' He lifted my arm, and rather clumsily I struggled up from my chair. But I did nothing to object or resist. I said nothing, and I kept my head down and swallowed the choking lump in my throat as I was led over the cool floor towards the bedrooms.

Chapter Fifteen

I stood like a little girl in the middle of his room. It was as simply furnished as ours, and the narrow single bed against the wall made the room seem even barer perhaps than the prisoner's quarters, strangely enough. The tears welled up in my eyes, and then trickled down my face. Automatically, I had folded my hands in front of my pubes in a pathetic gesture of coyness he did not fail to notice. His smile made me cringe with shame.

'Come now, no need for tears,' he said. 'I am simply going to fuck you, not hurt you.' I gaped at him. His harsh words were like a slap in the face. 'And you do not need to pretend to be shocked, Mrs Kinsella. I know how much you like to fuck and be fucked. I know about you and Krista, and you and Mrs Freeman. And I also know about you and the president,' he added. 'Yes, you like to fuck. Like all the other degenerate westerners I have met. So come, do what you like to do best and what you are so very good at.' He lay back on the narrow bed, his arms folded behind his head, and I knew what I had to do, and shamefully, without even an attempt at a protest, I obeyed him.

I moved slowly to kneel beside the bed. Teasingly, I drew down the zip of his fly, eased my fingers into the fold, and felt the pulsing shape of his cock within its tight concealment. I could just glimpse his underwear; black, but I could find no opening. I rubbed the outline of his stirring penis, felt the dome shape, the uncoiling length of his stiffening column. I let my fingers trace the shaft, and the smooth swell of his balls beneath it. Despite the awful predicament I was in, I could not help but secretly acknowledge how impressively it grew beneath my palm and fingers. I found the elastic of his briefs and plucked at the tightness, allowing the swollen head to emerge, like an animal from its lair. My fingertips were immediately slick with the slight discharge that came from the throbbing helm. I pushed down on the resisting material more determinedly, and at last the elastic dipped and the hotly fecund penis, together with its heavy testicles, came spilling over the edge of the skimpy garment.

He grunted, lifted his hips, and assisted me in easing down his trousers. I paused to slip off his shoes, and the light cotton socks, before removing his trousers altogether. I forced myself not to rush, not to be clumsy or timid. I would make damned sure he could not criticise me for not living up to the expectations he clearly had of me, and my sexual skills!

His prick was lolling now over the black material of his briefs. The rich bush of his black pubes, and the narrow line of hairs climbing up towards his belly button, stood out against the olive tone of his skin, and despite my loathing of the man and what he had, and was still, putting us all through, I felt the inner wetness of my own excitement deepening.

Carefully I slipped his underpants off, and then I reached up, and very slowly unbuttoned his shirt. Once again he assisted me, sitting up so that I could slide it from his smooth shoulders and place it carefully on top of the rest of his discarded clothing. The flat of my hands pressed against his chest, pushing him back onto the pillow. I lifted myself so that I hung over him, my red hair tumbling down to spill profusely over his flat stomach, against which I held his beautiful, pulsing penis, drinking in the intoxicating sexual odour of it.

With a shiver of delight I bent from the waist, grasped the warm column at the base of its swollen helm, and pushed firmly down, stretching the skin towards his balls, seeing the blood rush anew into the gleaming glans. I lapped gingerly at it, shivered again with that unique mixture of fear and desire at the sharp taste of his fluid, and then my tongue, bolder now, caressed the length of the throbbing column, and sucked in all the wonderful essence of his manhood that my body increasingly craved. I was close to coming, waiting only for the fulfilment of making love to this splendid creature who was consuming me with need.

Somehow I forced myself to cling to some measure of control. I climbed on the bed, straddled his thighs, but kept myself from lowering myself to meet that resplendent, rearing prick. Instead I lifted my bottom and dipped my head to his magnificent tool, licked and nibbled hungrily from the damp sac of his balls, up every millimetre of that vibrant column, and back to the swell of his smooth helm. I grasped him hard by the base of his shaft and stretched my lips wide, my hair tossing like wild flames about him as I strove to take as much of him as I could into my straining, worshipping mouth.

Then I jerked back as his hands fastened on my shoulders

and he turned me with ease, we rolled over, his thighs still inside mine. The breath was crushed from my lungs, his body pressing down on mine, sandwiching me between himself and the bed, and he penetrated me with one powerful thrust. My knees lifted in an instinctive effort to ease the drive of his flesh to my very centre. He rutted on top of me, consumed by his need to fuck me, until he gritted his teeth and exploded with a shattering force.

The shock and the fury of it had taken me by surprise, snatched and tossed me from my own private sensual fantasy into the whirlwind of his lust. Now, at the surging flood that claimed me, my own basic instinct shattered my senses and I responded, intent only on impaling myself on that elemental savagery, soaring with him, part of that whirlwind with him. I climbed, swept up like a graceful bird to the summit, hovered, and then burst into the brilliance of coming – timelessly, endlessly, so that I shuddered and clutched at him, screamed for such intensity to end, and screamed for it to go on for ever…

'You see, you are a very good fuck, I told you so.' His words penetrated my mind's drifting, and then I was alone on the bed. I heard him enter the shower next door, and then he was soon back, with a towel wrapped about his hips. 'Get cleaned up, and then get back to your husband,' he ordered coldly, and I crawled obediently away.

And the worst part of the episode was having to go back to the living room. I felt sullied and degraded, even though I tried to tell myself I was being ridiculous. In the past Jack had actively conspired in my fucking with other men, had actually watched me doing it on more than one occasion, so why should I feel so guilty and ashamed now? My answer was that, on all those other occasions it had been our choice. This time we were both totally helpless, compelled to go along with whatever our captors chose to do with us, or to us. And with this came the even more disturbing realisation that this utter submission was a powerful element in the sexual excitement my body was deriving from all this, an aphrodisiac headier than any I had previously known. It was an avenue I did not wish to explore further.

Uncannily in tune with my state of mind, Jack spoke to me as soon as I returned. 'All right, love?' he asked, staring closely and bright-eyed at me, the hint of a challenge in his look and his voice. 'Give him what he wanted, I hope?' he went on without too much conviction. 'We've got to keep the bugger sweet, eh? Especially now, when we're all they've got left.'

Thankfully, I did not have to respond because a distraction came in a series of rising yelps of pain from down the corridor, and then Jane's muffled pleas for mercy became audible. I looked in mute compassion at Carl, whose face was contorted with suffering as he gazed towards the doorway. I moved across and reached over to him, put my hand out to touch his arm, but he stepped back quickly, as though the proximity of my naked flesh was too much for him. He blushed deeply and turned away, so Jack and I started a pointless conversation in an effort to distract him from the sounds of the swishing blows and Jane's cries.

Thankfully, they soon died away, and there was a long period of silence while we strove not to listen for any further noises of punishment. The silence was broken by a sharp rapping, and then Khotan's voice called out with clear impatience, 'Krista! We have to get moving. Let us go! Now!'

He came into the room and we all stared at our feet guiltily, afraid of the silence but more afraid to break it. He did not look at me, but I wanted to die with shame when he said harshly to Jack, 'Your lovely wife knows her duties as a woman. You are a lucky man.'

Eventually Krista appeared, dressed in her usual military style, simple slacks and a bush shirt, yet she nevertheless managed to look very sexy and attractive, as always. She approached Carl, slipped her arm around his shoulders and pulled his slim body against her, like an older sister hugging her kid brother. Then she let her free hand drop and gave his penis a playful tug. 'There now, I hope that wife of yours will be a little sweeter for a while,' she goaded him. 'But you will have to be a little gentle if you play with her pussy.' She laughed, and then looked at Jack and me. 'And that goes for all of you.' And then with another patronising laugh, she followed her associate out to the waiting vehicle.

When I heard the shower running, I hastened down the corridor. The door was open, and Jane's red face was damp with the evidence of tears recently shed. She whimpered under the cleansing jet of water, and I saw the livid twin circles of blotchy flesh on her bottom, which she could hardly bear to touch they obviously hurt her so much.

Once showered, she winced and whimpered at my light dabs with the towel, and as I soothed her hot curves with cold cream as gently as I could. I was pretty well satiated after my recent experience, yet I felt that first quivering spasm of rejuvenating desire at contact with her lovely body. I turned her around and let our bodies rest together, let my thigh slide between hers, our hardened nipples brushing teasingly. But though she responded to my gentle kiss, her lips parting, our tongues intertwining, she eventually broke free with a shaky half sob, half laugh. 'No more, please, Moira. Not now. I don't think I could. Anyway, the boys will be waiting for us, and we shouldn't keep them waiting too long.'

Later that night, after a tense, interminable afternoon, the four of us lounged listlessly about the main room area. I could not bring myself to go off to the bedroom with Jack after the morning's activity, and I guess Jane felt the same way about her and Carl. We were trying to find some safe topics of conversation, and avoiding the one uppermost in our minds, when we heard the sound of an engine, and saw the headlamps sweeping across the blackness of the windows.

A few minutes later, the only person to enter was one of the hijackers, the one who had taken a shine to Carl. 'No one else come tonight,' he told us. 'But no matter, I have been sent to look after you.'

His words, and the evil smile that went with them, did nothing to ease our anxiety. But his gaze was directed towards Carl – then to her dismay, towards Jane as well. 'Come, you two,' he commanded, leering at them spitefully. 'We have early night, okay?' The dark eyes fixed on Jack and me. 'You two go to bed also. But jig-a-jig very quiet, yes? Let's go.'

In the strange privacy of the bedroom we climbed under the sheet in uneasy silence, unable to stop ourselves from listening for sounds from down the corridor. All we could hear was the deep rumble of the man's voice. We could not distinguish the words, but my brain was working overtime. It struck me again, despairingly, how utterly helpless we were, and how contemptuously they flung this fact in our faces the whole time. The very familiarity of our nakedness, to one another and to our captors, was a powerful sign of how submissive we had become, how meekly accepting of our humiliating condition. Out captors did not even carry guns, or weapons of any kind any longer with which to intimidate us. They did not need to. They left us alone for long periods during the day, and all night, every night. All they had done was tell us not to dare stick our noses outside the door, and we obeyed them without question.

We were like mice in a relatively comfortable cage. We did everything they told us, in blind obedience. They punished us, and used us for their sexual pleasure whenever they felt like it, and we submitted to this inhuman treatment without even a murmur of protest.

Like this morning, when they used Jane and me to satisfy their appetites while our husbands sat impotently in the outer room, and not only did we not say anything in protest, I at least actually enjoyed it. And right now, one of them was amusing himself with Carl and Jane, while Jack and I were packed off to bed like a couple of kids.

'We ought to do something,' I said, grabbing Jack's wrist. 'There's only one of them, and four of us. They're treating us with absolute contempt, as though we're hopeless and worthless, and that's exactly what we're becoming. It's awful! We have to do something! If we don't do something, I'll cease to respect myself completely! We can't keep behaving as though we're helpless.'

'But we *are* helpless.' The frankness of Jack's response pulled me up short. 'As far as they're concerned we count for nothing. And they're probably right.'

We were both speaking in whispers, lying huddled together on the bed.

'What do you think we can do?' he continued savagely. 'Suppose by some miracle we were able to overpower him in there, what could we do then? You think we could break out past the guards? With us naked and not so much as a catapult between us? And even if we managed that amazing feat, where would we go? Where the fuck are we? We don't even know that!'

He held me tight. 'That's just what we are, babe – hopeless and worthless. Don't ever forget it. We all belong to them, to do with what they will. You've got to remember that, and stop torturing yourself over it. We all have to remember that we're powerless if we want to come through this alive. So make the most of the chances they give us. We're together now, but that might change at any moment, so let's be glad about it while we have the chance.'

His fingers crept between my thighs and moved rhythmically, and my hips mirrored the gentle rhythm. I knew he was right. It wasn't our fault we found ourselves in this predicament. There was no point torturing myself with self-recrimination. I was simply doing what I had to do to survive. I reached down, seized his growing erection and parted my thighs wider, urging him to me.

Chapter Sixteen

I gazed down at the stubbly dome burrowing away between my parted thighs, and shivered with joy at the feathery strokes of the tongue, then the nipping bite of teeth on my opened labia. With a little squirm, part revulsion and part delight, I reached down and let my fingers caress its short, prickly growth. Carl thrust his face more avidly into my succulent wetness, his mouth worked with more conviction, taking my touch to be an encouragement for him to increase the urgency of his activity.

At the same instant Jane's mouth closed more firmly over my nipple and sucked hungrily, and I let myself go, moulding into the bountiful flesh wrapped all around me, my tummy lifting, thrusting back at Carl's face. I shuddered at the delicious force of the orgasm, letting it carry me on its flow, heightened by the feel of Jane's body pressing rhythmically against mine, and the knowledge of Jack's sleek penis driven deep into her cunt beneath those sweetly clenching buttocks of hers. A bottom which was as darkly barred as mine by the weals of the cruel whipping Krista had given us only two nights before, in front of the audience of our husbands and our three grinning male captors.

Yet, painful as it was, it signalled another important stage in the development of our lives as hostages – and it truly did feel like a lifetime since we had had any control over even the smallest act of our existence. Now we were given a significant freedom, for us, compared to what we had been put through, over our own bodies and what we were permitted to do with them. Of course we were still naked prisoners, and still utterly at our captors' mercy. Reminding us of this indelible fact was the point of Krista beating us, and I guess, of the weird three-way sex session between the hijacker, Carl and Jane, the bizarre details of which she confided in me a few days later. As if we needed any such reminders of our status!

But, after that beating, we were left alone to do as we wished much more often than not, and there seemed to be a new freedom about the building. I pondered this as I recovered from that wonderful orgasm, and gazed at our erotic combination of flesh.

It had occurred to me to wonder if in fact it was an extra degree of freedom at all, or was it merely another demonstration of their power over us that they no longer had to watch over us to make sure we behaved exactly as they wanted us to?

Whatever the reason, our captors were thankfully abusing us less and less frequently. And even their visits to the compound became more and more infrequent, and more fleeting as well. One or two of the guards would look in briefly, once or twice a day, and then we would see no more of them until the next day. It was now unusual for Krista or the other two hijackers to spend a night there with us, and as for my sexual encounter with Khotan, that was never repeated even though I know he really enjoyed screwing me.

As time passed slowly, our cocooned existence was oddly undisturbed, and timeless almost, and gradually I grew to like Carl more and more, and took it upon myself to help bring him further out of the shell he all too easily hid in.

One morning, I slipped into the shower room after him. He jumped when he saw me appear there in the cubicle with him.

'You're not going to get away this time,' I whispered seductively. My blood was surging with an altogether new, savage excitement. The unaccustomed thrill of dominance flowed through me, and caused my sex to throb with an intense desire. It was wonderful. I reached for him and began to lather his body with soap, from his chest down to his waist, his hips, to that jutting cock of his, which beat and quivered in my tight grasp.

Slowly, savouring to the full my power and the thrill it gave me, I sank to my knees beneath the cascading water, let my hand fondle and clutch his buttocks, let my soapy fingers dig deep into the tight valley, and then feel the hardness of his anus. One of my fingers, slick with soap, probed, and pushed boldly into the clutch of his sphincter, forcing it to yield to me. His buttocks hollowed, he gave a convulsive shudder from head to toe, and his hips moved forward to push his straining erection into my face. I let it rub against my cheek, and then moved and let it slide over my brow, and pass down over my lips, before I peeled them open and took him into my eager mouth. I sucked him deeply, tasting the strong lather, drawing in the living thickness until I captured it entirely, its beating strength pressing against the roof of my mouth and the back of my throat.

He was sighing, his hands clutched the streaming, darkened strands of my hair, which clung to my brow, and cheeks, and shoulders. I could feel him shuddering as I held him to me. 'No, no, please,' he mumbled without conviction, and I knew that this was it. I pulled my mouth clear, seized his bobbing erection in both hands, and pressed it to my upturned face. He jerked, his hips grinding, and the thick bounty of his come erupted onto me, spilling over my lips and chin, oozing into my hair, and I felt his cock immediately losing its powerful rigidity.

He slumped to the puddles on the tiles and I cradled him, lifting my face to the cleansing water, letting it wash his semen from me while I held him close.

Chapter Seventeen

On reflection, I was more than a little ashamed of the special relationship growing between Carl and me. Just as I had suspected, despite his instance of the opposite, Carl's nature was such that the slight degree of dominance I introduced allowed him to feel comfortable with himself even as he thoroughly enjoyed submitting to me. The shower room became our special rendezvous, but only on rare occasions. Of course, the other two suspected what was going on. Jack even teased me about it, in that mocking way of his, whereas Jane simply ignored it. We all seemed to know that any conflict between us would be dangerous while we were living in such an unnaturally confined proximity.

We knew nothing of what was happening in the world we had been snatched from. We had no contact with the guards, who slouched around the hot and dusty compound day after day, looking thoroughly bored. We saw them as distant menacing figures through the windows, and we were only too glad that they kept their distance.

We spent hour after hour discussing what had happened to us already, and speculating on what might happen to us in the future. I thought a lot about Nicky and Anita. Had they really been freed, along with all the others, as we had been told they were? Were we four really the only hostages left? And if so, why? It did not seem at all fair.

Our ordeal had been going on for about seven months now. Not only was it unfair, it was utterly baffling and I could not get my head round why we were still being held, and I knew my other three fellow captives felt the same way. Would they ever let us go? We had no idea.

Yet, oddly enough, we no longer feared for our lives. We were still afraid – of Krista's unjust punishments, and that sheer boredom might turn the guards rogue – but since our removal from the airport buildings, we had had the feeling that we were not in mortal danger. This feeling had come as a blessed relief, to say the least. But what then was to be our fate? To remain forever in this state of limbo, naked slaves who had no control over our lives at all?

Sometimes, paradoxically, the thought of release itself scared me. I never voiced my fears, but they kept recurring. There was something insidiously seductive and sexually arousing about our total helplessness and submission. We had no decisions to make, no need to exert our will, no choices to ponder. Our lives consisted simply in just doing what we were told, and satisfying our basic needs and desires and instincts. In the wake of such moments of reflection, I was scourged with self-disgust. My conscience berated me for thinking such perversely contented thoughts, for we were being kept in a stifling sweatbox, fed and watered by captors who held us completely and contemptuously in their power.

On the other hand, there would be a whole new ball game out there, when, and if, the day of our release ever came. I could not believe that, out of all the hostages who had been held for those endless weeks in the airport building, there would not be at least one who would reveal all the lurid details of that phase of our captivity – the nudity, the physical degradations, the beatings – and the lesbian exploits Krista had indulged in with her 'harem'. Even Nicky might have been tempted to spill the beans, or rather, open the can of worms. And what a tale she would have to tell, if she could overcome the shame she must surely feel at having her story making headlines around the world. Robbed of her virginity, twice – at the hands of Krista and then by no less a person than the President of Leontondo himself and his three stalwart cronies.

The repercussions throughout the world media must surely be tremendous. Which was why I was beginning to feel increasingly uneasy about the prospect of release.

But little did I know that things were about to change for us yet again.

And the change came, as always, with unexpected suddenness.

One afternoon we were lounging around, hot and bored as usual, when we heard yelling and the running of feet and the roar of what sounded like a convoy of vehicles. We stood and looked anxiously out of the windows at a retinue of impressively senior-looking army personnel, and then we moved out onto the veranda, where they confronted us.

The most senior, a man nearly as large as Koloba, pointed directly at me. 'Come,' he said gruffly, and without ceremony he snatched me by the wrist. 'You are wanted.'

I had time for one last despairing glance back at Jack, who stood motionless with Jane and Carl, but I suspected it would be wise not to protest. With my slender wrist clamped in his powerful grasp I followed him down the wooden steps, somewhat carefully because of the heat and the stabbing prickles of gravel beneath my bare feet.

Everything served to remind me of the nakedness I had grown accustomed to for so long. The plastic of the vehicle's seat was almost painfully hot on my bottom and the backs of my thighs as I sat down on it. The clothing of the large man and the driver brushed against my skin, for I sat squashed in the front between them. My heart was still racing. Where were they taking me – and why? It was extremely alarming, but like the perfect slaves we had all become, I said nothing.

After a hot and bumpy ride of several miles along a track we came to a grassy clearing, where more guards were waiting. In the centre of the clearing was a small helicopter, in the same drab military green as the vehicles, its rotor blades spinning slowly. We got out of the Land Rover and I realised I was being led towards it. My knees were like jelly. This surely meant I was being taken some distance. Were they going to set me free? Why had they separated me from the others?

'Come,' the large man said again, and struggling to hold back the tears of fear and sudden solitude from being separated from the others, who had been my only solace during this endless ordeal, I climbed aboard the helicopter, too distraught to worry about the inelegant picture I must have presented scrabbling into the small glass bubble. The pilot was already sitting in his place, and I was vaguely aware of another crewmember crouched with his back to me in the rear of the small cockpit, but I didn't really take too much notice. The large man leaned in, grinned broadly, and with an even greater sense of panic I realised he was not coming with us.

'Please, for security,' was all he said as he leaned in closer and slipped a black eye mask over my head, condemning me to darkness. At once I recalled the weird game played at the palace, when the four of us girls had been blindfolded and screwed, and I had distinguished myself by being the only one to guess who my partner had been.

Oddly enough, being deprived of sight was curiously calming. I sank back, giving myself up to the helplessness of my position. I felt firm hands touching me, lifting me slightly and slipping a broad canvas strap between my thighs, clipping it to a belt around my hips. It chafed against my sensitive skin as the motor coughed, and then clattered and roared into life. My belly hollowed, seemed to fall away, and I knew we were airborne. I leant back, trembling, my mind incapable of any constructive thought.

I don't know how long I remained thus, before I felt strong fingers pressing on the buckle at my tummy, releasing me from the harness, and then easing me from my seat. We were flying on an even keel, and I was placed in a kneeling position across the bucket seat, raising my hips. Was I going to be screwed me in mid-air, on the way to wherever it was I was going?

The hands felt rough, and I assumed they had to belong to the figure who had been sitting behind me. They cradled my breasts, stroked my nipples until they became erect, tingling with sensation. His lips touched my neck, lifting the thick red hair to plant light kisses on my skin that made me shiver, and stirred those pulses of desire I could not deny. He turned my head, his tongue probing into my mouth, which opened obediently, and then I felt his weight enveloping me, felt the solid girth of his belly resting on my lower back.

The fingers ferreted between my thighs, explored the cleft of my behind, and found the moistening lips of my labia. They parted the slick tissue, opening me, and relentlessly arousing me until I was gasping with need and my bottom was thrusting back against his bulk, begging for satisfaction.

'Please,' I sobbed, and felt the tears soaking the material padded against my eyes. Still the fingers probed. I felt one insert itself into the entrance of my vagina, and slide slowly inward, claiming the narrow sheath that hugged it hungrily. I was whimpering now, my head hanging low, twisting from side to side, and pleading for him to go on.

Just when I was sure I could stand it no more and was ready to plunge over the chasm of my climax, the finger withdrew. Those sturdy hands pressed at my thighs, inching them wider apart, and at last came the blessed touch of his cock, the slippery helm of an erect penis nudging into my tight flesh. Its entry into me was slow, controlled, until my whole writhing frame was a mass of quivering hunger. The joy was almost too great to endure. My bottom lifted and thrust back against that driving force, and I cried at the burst of my coming, on and on, wave after wave until I slumped exhausted, absorbing his piston-like lunges to my very centre until he too was spent.

I crouched there, sobbing, curled under his bulk while he rested in me, slowly shrinking out of me. I could not move – I did not want to move.

'Welcome aboard,' a deep, familiar voice growled close to my ear. The blindfold was taken off and there was Koloba's grinning face next to my own, my eyes confirming what my body already knew.

Then I gasped again in genuine wonder, for there, through the glass against which my sweating features and pale body were pressed, lay a breathtaking panorama of Leontondo's capital, its green clad hills and splendid buildings and, in the far distance, the shimmering surface, aflame with the late sun, of the Great Lake, where our adventure had begun.

Chapter Eighteen

'Doesn't she look sexy, Kamau?' The helicopter pilot, who had shown remarkable discipline in keeping his eyes fixed firmly ahead while his president had been sporting over his shoulder with a naked white female, now permitted himself a swift glance in my direction. He nodded and smiled, and paradoxically, I felt myself blushing, now that I was, for the first time in many months, fully clothed. True, what I was wearing was not quite what I would have chosen for myself, but after a short period when I sat beside the president while we flew in a breathtaking tour over the capital, he had delved into a bag beneath his seat, produced a bundle, and thrust it in my lap with orders for me to get dressed right away.

It didn't take long for me to obey. In the bag I discovered a camouflage suit of baggy trousers and jacket, a pair of black canvas shoes, and a floppy brimmed, olive bush hat. There were no undies. The suit swamped me and the plimsolls were too big, but at least it was clothing. It was strange to feel the cloth on my skin after all this time, and to have my body hidden from view.

'You look like a boy soldier,' the president chortled. Not quite, I thought, as my long hair tumbled about my shoulders from beneath the floppy hat, but I didn't argue. I was still dazed by all that had happened to me within the last hour or so, and from the novelty of no longer being naked. The horizon to the east was already darkening, and we left the lights of the twinkling city below as we swung away towards the blaze of sunset over the lake. In a few minutes we were descending rapidly, and I thought I recognised the shape of the palace where the president had 'entertained' Jane and me and the other two girls – months before, I reflected.

But this was an altogether different arrival. We touched down on the front lawn, before the shallow curve of white steps that led to the imposing entrance. There was a small delegation of black figures waiting to greet us, and Koloba himself helped me down from the helicopter, and then held my hand as he led me inside and introduced me to a smartly dressed entourage, some in military uniforms and some – the palace staff, I later discovered – in civilian clothes.

'This is Mrs Kinsella,' he told them. 'She is to be our guest for a few days.' Mrs Kinsella, and his *guest?* My brain reeled. It was a dream from which I dreaded waking.

But it was not a dream. Koloba held my hand, guiding me over the polished floor of the grand hall, and up the wide red-carpeted staircase. Minutes later I was standing in a magnificently appointed bedroom, and a pretty girl in a maid's outfit of black dress and white apron, including the saucy scrap of white lace pinned to her curly head, was bobbing respectfully before me.

'This is Awina,' the president told me. 'She will look after you. She will get you anything you want. Relax now, and have a bath. You will find clothes in the wardrobe. I hope they are your size. I think they are. Dinner is at eight. It will be with just a few friends, nothing formal. I will send someone to fetch you for drinks in a couple of hours. Now, make yourself at home.'

I stared after him. There was so much I wanted to ask, but my brain just would not function clearly.

'Shall I run your bath, memsa'ab?' the pretty maid asked me.

I blinked at the girl. 'Erm – yes, please, Awina,' I mumbled, unable to believe I was being waited on. I had been treated like a slave for months, and now here I was giving someone instructions to draw me a bath! I was possessed by an overwhelming sense of unreality.

My maid gave me a dazzling smile and headed for an adjoining door, through which I saw a bathroom as resplendent as the one where the president had frolicked with Jane and me. Utterly confused, not entirely certain I was not dreaming, I slipped off the unflattering clothes and wandered after the maid. The poor girl's eyes widened and she looked embarrassed when she saw my naked body, but she said nothing, merely turned quickly to busy herself with the fragrant foam in the large tub.

'It is ready, memsa'ab,' she said. 'You want me to stay with you?'

'Yes please, stay and talk to me.' I felt I needed her there, to help me cling to some semblance of reality.

It was hard, though, and the same dreamlike quality enveloped me when I surveyed the silk underwear in the drawers, and the blouses, skirts, and dresses hanging in abundance in the vast wardrobe. I studied myself in the full length mirrors with a new awareness, let the fluffy white towel fall at my feet, titillated by the shy, surreptitious stares of Awina. Then I chose a matching set of bra and

French knickers of a tasteful deep ivory and made of a fine satin that felt soft as a caress, and a dress of elegant simplicity that hugged my curves tastefully and reached only to mid-thigh.

When the president returned, his eyes conveyed the same message of lust I had seen before, though this time he disguised it with a gallantry of behaviour that added strongly to my sense of disbelief and unreality. What is more, his attention never wavered from me despite the presence of several other women, all African, some of quite outstanding beauty and sophistication. True, they all had male escorts, though I was sure that would be no deterrent to the president if he wished to pursue matters with one of them.

All of this could not be happening! I kept recalling our previous visit to the palace, and how utterly slavish our status and treatment had been then. Now, perfumed and dressed in the finest clothes, I sat at an elegant table where I was waited upon, and wined and dined as an honoured guest, at the right hand of the president himself.

The president who, some hours later, came to my bedroom and made love to me. Made love! As though I was a person in my own right, not some sex slave whose only worth lay in being there for the taking whenever he chose.

I wondered why all this was happening, and sobbed like a child when he held me tenderly in the darkness, as tenderly as the lover into which he had miraculously transformed himself.

He was still in my bed the next morning. His large hands were touching me with astounding gentleness and skill, even as I awoke, my blood already racing with the need he created in me, and satisfied. Once more his great bulk descended on me, his potency spearing me to a swift and tumultuous climax. Only then did I feel the crushing weight of him, the broad plane of his back on which my hands rested, the stout thighs where my heels lay. He groaned, levered himself off me, the bed sinking as he rolled off me to lie by my side.

'Hmmm,' he growled with satisfaction, 'you are very good, *very* good, you know. I will miss you terribly. Will you not come and be my wife number three?'

'I'm already married,' I answered, my voice trembling, not really capturing the strength of tone I was after. I hesitated, not sure I wanted to ask the question that begged to be asked. The words almost stuck in my throat. 'W-why, Mr President… where am I going?'

He looked amused, his eyes sparkling with mischief. 'You are going home, of course,' he answered simply. 'In a few days from now, you will be free. And what will you tell the world about me, I wonder?'

My heart hammered and now I could scarcely get my breath. All at once I knew the full significance of his question. With an intuitive leap, I understood why I had been brought to the palace. I said, as calmly as I could, 'But what about the others? What is going to happen to them?' My voice shook a little, but I forced myself to ask, 'Are they also going to be released?'

Now it was his turn to pause briefly, and it was a pause I was all too conscious of. 'Of course, my dear,' he said, his voice rich and deep. 'You will all go free. At least, I sincerely hope so. Though the thought of losing you makes me almost wish I could hold you here forever.' And once more he gathered me into his bulk, his lips seeking mine. Tensely I waited, those qualifying words of his, 'I sincerely hope so', echoing in my head. There was some sort of bargain to be struck, I was sure of that. What was it he wanted of me?

He was clearly in no hurry to pursue his plan, and as for me, I was still too timid and bemused by the dramatic change in my fortune to try to push things along, as much as part of me wanted to.

I had another leisurely soak in fragrant suds after he left me. Awina brought in a breakfast tray. I sat at a small table set in front of the tall windows where the warm morning sun poured over me, and I could see the brilliant green of the lawn, the foliage of carefully landscaped trees, and beyond it, the distant hazy shimmer of the lake. It wasn't until Awina hurried forward, the half veiled shock evident in her expression, that I realised I had sat down naked. She slipped the creamy satin robe about my shoulders and I covered myself, tying the sash tightly at my waist. 'Thanks,' I smiled at her. 'I've been so used to going around naked for so long, I forgot myself.'

The president had told me we would be going on another helicopter journey, over some of the huge game reserves, so after the meal, with Awina's help, I chose an impeccable safari suit of pale linen. The slacks, with their knife-edge creases, hugged my slender frame quite alluringly, I thought, and again I marvelled at how accurately the measurements of my newly acquired wardrobe had been chosen. The short-sleeved jacket's belted waist also emphasised my slenderness.

I was surprised to find that that no guards were to accompany us, only his pilot, Kamau, who had witnessed our lewd congress in the skies over the city. Once more I felt myself blushing at his polite smile and greeting when we climbed aboard. This time there was to be no repeat of such indecorous behaviour, however. After a fascinating low-level flight picking out and tracking many species of big game, we landed at a remote spot to picnic from the excellent lunch basket provided for us. There was even chilled wine and iced beer included in the gourmet repast. And then I spied a familiar expression spreading across the president's shining face.

'Keep a watch, Kamau,' he said to his pilot. 'I do not want a rhino's horn up my bottom!' And he grabbed my hand, and led me off out of sight through the dead-looking thorn scrub behind a big red anthill. 'Let's jig-a-jig, my little red *malaya*.' He smiled fondly down at me.

Malaya. Prostitute. The idea excited me; better a prostitute than a slave, I told myself. Prostitutes are paid for what they do. What would my payment be? Freedom? Then I suddenly felt an unexpected lurch of real trepidation. Was I ready for the world that was waiting to claim me again? Suddenly I was swamped with a feeling of emptiness, and I found myself inexplicably yearning for my old state of total submission. I thought of my other three fellow captives, pictured them back at the compound, and wanted desperately to be with them again.

The president's urgent hands on my clothing distracted me from my longing. He was fumbling under my jacket, unbuckling my trousers, unzipping them and easing them down over my hips. They clung around my safari boots, and he would not be able to get them off unless he removed my footwear first. But already he had pushed me to my knees, and then forward, so that my hands rested in the dry dust. I felt his fingers as he dragged my white knickers down, leaving them to cling around my thighs. I felt vulnerable, my pale rump exposed to the burning sun, the loosened clothing tight around me like bonds.

He was kneeling behind me, and I glanced over my shoulder to see what he was doing. He fumbled at his fly, hauled out his thick penis, spearing up from his groin. The dome was slimy with emission as he guided it into my buttock cleft. I felt the cold smears and tensed, lifting my bottom slightly as his prick nosed into the soft valley, and located the dewy soft lips of my sex at the base of the divide. A thumb and forefinger prised me open, and he pushed into me, so slowly that I shivered as I savoured every centimetre of the inexorable penetration.

Grunting, my head down, my red hair sweeping the dust between my spread hands, I thrust my bottom back against his ramming bulk, impaling myself, and he began the rhythmic driving, his huge frame fitting over my curving shape. His left hand crept round my hip and his fingers played through the damp tendrils of my pubes, then found the uppermost folds of my labia, teased and rolled them. A pad slid under their spongy tissue, stretched the slippery skin until my clit began to pulse with the force of the excitement coursing through me. 'Oh!' I sobbed, rocking furiously, buffeting my buttocks onto the slabs of his thighs. 'I'm coming!' I wailed, threshing so that he had to hold me tight and pin me against him in the frenzied jerks of my climax.

My head dipped, my brow rested on the ground, in the dust, and I felt the heaving mass of him fold over me while his weapon screwed mercilessly to my very centre. I whimpered with relief at the surging flood of his coming inside me.

That evening Koloba shared the spacious bath with me, dismissing Awina with a frankly lecherous wink. 'I will attend to Memsa'ab Moira tonight,' he grinned. 'And you must call me Elias, that is my name,' he told me, when the maid had left us alone together.

'Dress carefully for dinner,' Elias instructed me when we finally managed to prise ourselves apart and dry ourselves. 'We have a distinguished guest. No less a person than the British ambassador himself.'

So this was it! Now things were really moving, and could never be the same again. I felt sick with conflicting emotions and nerves, and had to screw my courage to its utmost to force myself to walk down that imposing staircase to the reception. I had heeded Koloba's instructions; wearing an off the shoulder full-length evening gown, severely cut to mould my shapely figure, in the deepest of burgundies. With Awina's help I had brushed my hair until it glowed lustrously and hung in a haloing cloud of richness about my face and shoulders. I made no attempt to pin it up or restrain it, and I had my reward when I saw the admiring looks of the assembled crowd in the dining room. Even the patrician features of Sir Gordon Wills, trained in diplomacy as he was, could not disguise a glance of appreciation as I was introduced to him. His voice was rich, like a well-matured brandy, soothing, and warm, and I felt my tummy respond to it.

'Ah, Mrs Kinsella,' he crooned, 'you look absolutely lovely, my dear. Quite amazing, after all you've been through.'

Thereafter the evening seemed to unfold in a somewhat surreal manner; there were no other women present, and those gathered for dinner were only a few of the president's closest aides. I was a British subject, and here was the representative of my government, sitting at my side sharing the table with the man who was responsible for keeping me and others, including my husband, prisoner. With such thoughts confusing me it was hard even to follow the polite conversations going on all around the table.

There was no getting over the fact that it was all a little too weird for me to feel at ease. Koloba, it must be clear to the whole world by now, was as much our kidnapper as Krista and the gang. From the very beginning his soldiers had taken over guard duties, enabling the hijackers to come and go as they pleased. And yet, I realised with growing disbelief, Sir Gordon was treating him as if he were our saviour, as if he personally had saved our lives, snatched us from the jaws of death at the hijackers' hands.

The crunch came, though, a little later in the comfortable library, when only the president and Sir Gordon and me were present.

'Things are poised rather delicately,' Sir Gordon stated smoothly, addressing me. 'We haven't given in to your kidnappers, but we've made some significant concessions, all in the strictest confidence, of course. There's no need for you to know the details, but as I'm sure you can guess, negotiations have been going on for months. Considerable measures have been taken to ensure your safety and eventual return. The president,' he turned with a practised politician's smile towards the grinning host, and I felt a disturbing surge of fury which took even me by surprise, 'has been tireless in his efforts for your release...'

As I listened to his rhetoric I wanted to scream at him. Did he know, for example, that one of the president's tireless efforts was to have us brought to this very palace, upstairs somewhere, and have us used as entertainment for him and his cronies? And did he know that just two days before he had blindfolded me and fucked me whilst flying in a helicopter over the capital city? I wanted to shout this at the urbane statesman, but I remained silent. Months of captivity, punctuated by the occasional but quite painful punishment, had taught me to hold my tongue... well, at least when it came to asking questions and defending myself verbally. I had learned that if I wanted to remain comfortable, and not have a backside covered with uncomfortable welts, there were better uses to which I could put my tongue.

'The problem is,' Sir Gordon went on, 'that there has been so much speculation. Such wild rumours flew about after the release of the other hostages, especially the American girl and the stewardess. One thing we have had to give our word on is that we will suppress publicity as much as possible when you and the rest of your companions are finally released. Even the president's role in the affair has been called into serious question. There has been so much made of the fact that Leontondese military were used to guard you, when in fact it was the only way President Koloba could guarantee your safety.'

Nice one, Mr President, I thought, but still I made no comment.

'We thought you could exert your influence over your husband, and Mr and Mrs Freeman…'

Of course! For the first time since I had been whisked away by the presidential helicopter, I experienced a glimmer of understanding, which to my confused mind and emotions felt precious as gold. The president plucks me up in the air, literally, flies me off to his palace, pampers me and dresses me in silk lingerie and all the rest, and I fall swooning at his feet ready to do whatever he asks of me. It was such an obvious ploy I felt disgusted with myself for not having seen through it sooner. And yet, to be fair to myself, after months of wandering around naked, deprived of all but the most basic creature comforts, and rutting like an animal with every one and any one who wanted me, was it any wonder I had succumbed to the dream-like spell of silks and satins and scented baths and gourmet meals I could enjoy with my clothes on? 'Well, needless to say I can't answer for how the others feel,' I said finally. 'Some awful things – some very terrible things – have been done to us. Not just to Jane and me, mind you, but to the men as well.' My voice faded and I felt saddened as I thought of them still back in that sweltering hot compound probably worried sick about what had become of me.

'There is something else that might help persuade you.' The president's abrupt tone contrasted with the ambassador's clipped diplomacy. 'You had better see this before anyone else does. Khotan and the German girl, the two brains behind the hijack and the kidnapping, have copies of what I am about to show you, and they are threatening to release them if you do not cooperate.'

My stomach churned with dread, instantly understanding. Unable to move, I sat in the plush armchair watching in horror as he moved over to a television and switched it on along with a video recorder. My fears had been justified. There we were, all four of us; Jack and Jane, her limbs interlaced about his, Carl's head buried between my thighs… Jane and me in the shower… Carl and me in the shower…

The cruelly beautiful images went on, blurred and dissolved in the tears of defeat, humiliation, and acquiescence flooding down my cheeks in front of the shocked British ambassador.

Chapter Nineteen

Of course, they knew damned well they had me just where they wanted me, from the moment those explicit images appeared on the screen I was theirs to command again.

'Turn it off, please,' I said quietly, feely utterly defeated and degraded.

Sir Gordon recovered himself quickly and his voice was as silky smooth as ever. 'Of course, my dear, I understand what terrible pressures you were put under to provide those pictures. But I'm afraid the world media will not be quite so sympathetic in their treatment of you. They could very likely make your lives intolerable after your release, and you will find yourself exchanging one form of captivity for another. Life in the disapproving public eye can be quite a strain,' he warned, and then shrugged philosophically. 'I do think, however,' he went on impassively, 'that the kidnappers can probably be persuaded to keep it all quiet. But unfortunately the newshounds will be after you as soon as you reappear no matter what. They are like sharks following the scent of blood.

'So we thought we might offer you some kind of protection. We though it might be best for you and your companions to ease your return to the real world by spending time at a kind of retreat for a whole, to give you a chance to rehabilitate yourselves before you pick up your lives again.'

I sat there miserably, tortured by the shocking scenes we had just witnessed. At that moment I would have agreed to anything, agreed to go anywhere. But they didn't rush things, the president and the ambassador. After Sir Gordon took his leave, as phlegmatically charming as ever, Koloba took me up to bed once more – and a night as intense as the previous one had been promptly ensued. But there was a subtle difference, which grew less subtle as the long night progressed. He was still a casual lover screwing me, but now there was an easy possessiveness, a hint of his former mastery, which had been on full display when he had used the others and me purely as objects of gratification. And, ashamed though I am to admit it, there was that same response from my own treacherously submissive body; a deep desire that welcomed the very subservience that degraded me.

I only stirred in the first grey light of dawn – we had not been asleep very long – to feel the president's bulk rolling out from beside me. 'Duty calls, my little *malaya*,' his deep voice rumbled. 'You may go back to sleep, but I still have a country to run.' He chuckled.

When I surfaced from a dreamless sleep again it was, I felt, hours later and the room was full of the sunlight filtering in through the long drapes. Again I felt the mattress moving beside me, and still drifting sensuously up through the receding layers of sleep, I turned expecting to see the large man had returned.

'Hello Moira.'

I looked up and was stunned. I struggled up onto my elbows, my mouth open as I gazed in disbelief at Krista's smiling features! I could not believe I was awake, but then the reality of what I was seeing was confirmed as she sank down beside me on the bed and kissed me passionately. I fell back down into the softness of the pillow and the mattress, her feminine weight moulding to me, her tongue sinking into my mouth and possessing me until I gurgled weakly in my throat for mercy.

Her body lay along mine, every inch making sensual contact with my own. 'You look surprised,' she mused, after the long, lingering kiss she had bestowed upon me after our long separation. 'You did not think you had seen the last of me, did you? I could not leave without saying goodbye properly.' The seductiveness of her tone sent shivers of longing and apprehension through me. 'I have already said my goodbyes to Jane,' she went on. 'And now it is your turn.'

The uneasiness in my eyes undoubtedly made her glow with satisfaction, and when my gaze darted towards the door, she chuckled in a feminine version of the president's low, gratified laughter. 'Oh, don't worry, my pretty,' she purred sweetly. 'We will not be disturbed. I have got as long as I want with you.' She eased aside a little and peeled the bedclothes clear off my naked body, and I saw then that her clothes were neatly folded beside the bed. This was no secret, clandestine visit. The president was obviously aware of what was happening and was keeping well clear of the scene. But despite my concerns, my body trembled with that frisson of excitement Krista always inspired – and it was not to be disappointed.

I made no attempt at all to put up any resistance against her. Not that I could have summoned up the necessary will, either physically or in spirit. She took hold of my arms and I let her pinion my wrists to the bedrail above me with a short length of silk cord she had brought for the purpose, and it was not until she began to make teasing love to me that I discovered how securely she had tied me, for instinctively I sought to respond, to return the passion of the embraces she lavished on my captive flesh, only to feel the bite of the bonds on my skin as I strained to move my arms.

She was wickedly tender at first, holding herself away from me, allowing contact only at our hungry lips, nuzzling and nibbling in the first gentle bites of love. With infinite slowness her mouth worked down the length of my body, from my throat to the rise of my breasts, my nipples swelling with their need to be caressed, a need she instinctively satisfied as her lips closed over those upstanding buds of desire in turn. Then on down she went over the hollow of my belly, her tongue riming the shallow little eye of my navel, before proceeding over the quivering paleness leading to my uppermost chestnut curls, and the swell of the mound where my sex cleft clamoured for her attention.

But she made me wait until my frame writhed and twisted, lifting hungrily off the bed, my thighs squirming in that desperate need for fulfilment. While I struggled with my need, her mouth went on devouring me, inch by inch, moving over my thighs where the muscles locked, down to my knees, my shins, my ankles, and even my wriggling toes. And then up again she came, all the way up that trail of yearning hunger. Lost to everything except my need for her, I wept and begged for release. Not from the bonds, which were biting unnoticed into my tethered wrists, but the merciless gnawing at my very centre, which ran with its insatiable demand for her conquest. The tears poured from me, soaking the hair at my temples. She lay on top of me, every inch of her shapely frame moulding to mine, and I thrust up in desperate appeal. It was an age of sweet torture, then at last that lovely mouth bore down again, this time assisted by those knowing fingers, which peeled me open, laid bare that throbbing core to the ecstasy of her consuming tongue and teeth and lips. She ate into the very heart of me and I exploded, flooded, fragmented, with a blissful power beyond any means of expression.

Floating, above time, I drifted back through cloud layers of utter contentment to the reality of her comforting weight across my legs; her breath fanning the wet strands of hair that crowned my lower tummy, her cheek pressing against the top of my thigh, her fingers, still sticky with my fluids, toying absently with my pale nipples. I felt her turn me over onto my front, knew what was about to happen, dimly embraced the pain of the punishment which somehow seemed so fitting after such a total and willing surrender, even while my muscles tensed and the cheeks of my bottom hollowed with the anticipation of the scorching fire they were about to imbibe.

She used a thin belt this time, lashing my quivering flesh with a slow appreciation that was an integral part of her own consummation. The branding fire of the first sharp cut rippled through me. I buried my face in the smothering softness of the pillow, stretched my mouth wide in a silent scream and bit savagely into the material, choking the cries of pain in a kind of helpless tribute, and acknowledgement of my victim's role in her subjugation of me. The fire rippled again and again, and I felt my tautened flesh scoured, felt the ridges of pain-seared tissue standing up, vivid, scarlet emblems of the conqueror and the conquered, joining us as intimately and powerfully as the sexual union we had just shared. The pain rose and possessed me until I could no longer contain it. I lifted my flushed visage from the pillow and screamed, the cries torn from my inner spirit, blind howls which were, in their way, mirrors of the screams of ecstasy her loving had torn from me only minutes earlier.

The steady throb of the torment beat through to my swooning senses, telling me that the ordeal was over. She knelt, once more a lover, and then sat astride my legs and I could feel the seeping wetness at her satin crotch. And it was as a lover now that she finally rose, moved away, returned with a blessedly cool towel she had soaked in water, and dabbed at the burning weals standing up in scarlet stripes across my bottom.

I lay on my front, unable to move, and heard the soft rustle of her clothing as she dressed. She did not attempt to turn me over onto my back, which would have been cruel indeed, only lifted my head a little, and tenderly brushed the damp swirls of hair away from my neck and cheek to make room for the gentle kisses she rained down on them, before capturing my mouth for one last embrace.

'Goodbye,' she breathed huskily. 'Do not forget me.'

I lay still, apart from the involuntary trembling, the sobs

gradually dying until my tears stopped seeping from my eyes, the pain a dull throb of acceptance.

'No way! They're not buying me off so fucking easily!'

I cringed at Jack's vehement words and the belligerent thrust of his red face towards mine. The discomfort in my aching bottom reminded me it was only two days since I had endured the thrashing, and the final farewell loving, from Krista. Was it really possible she had no more control over our lives? And yet we were far from free, I was sure of that. In some ways I could scarcely explain to myself I felt we would never be free again.

I studied the elegant slacks, the smart shirt I was wearing, and the designer safari boots. And underneath, I appreciated the soft caress of real silk underwear. Across from me, Jane and Carl and Jack also looked strangely glamorous in their new and expensively cut clothing.

A deep resentment welled up in me at Jack's intransigence. He knew well enough what I had gone through in the eventful week during which I had been separated from him. He had seen the livid marks of my chastisement by Krista, and knew without asking how I had played the president's concubine. Surely he too, like the rest of us, should still be bemused at the good fortune that had so swiftly fallen upon us? The fine clothes, the sumptuous food and the luxurious surroundings, after all those months of privation and uncertainty? But no, apparently he was not at all bemused, and I was caught partly admiring and partly pulling my hair out in exasperation at the way he could so easily adapt to every dramatic change. Just the relief of seeing him and the others again, at being reunited, had reduced me to sobs of gratitude.

Later, when I faced Jack across the large silk covered double bed, in the guestroom to which we had been ceremonially escorted, I blushed like a virgin bride recalling all that had happened to me in the period since I'd last seen him – the amazing mid-air encounter in the helicopter, the nights of passion with Koloba, and the shockingly wonderful dawn of love with Krista. They stood as a great chasm between us – until Jack flung himself on me, with no more than a growl of happy lust, feverishly undressing me and shedding his own newly acquired clothes, to push me back onto the bed, to spread my legs wide to his rampant repossession of me. I was gasping in breathless excitement as his lovely rigid cock thrust its way to the hilt in my wet and willing tightness.

'You missed me?' he grinned, minutes later, when he lifted his sweating face to mine after our simultaneous climax. I was speechless, helpless to cover the enormity of the gulf between us.

And so it had been, in the hours that had passed since then.

'You must relax,' the president told all four of us, while I meekly stared red-faced down at the carpet, cringing with embarrassing memories of the things we had done together. 'I hope your accommodation will suffice,' he went on. 'Your troubles are over now. You are safe. Please – enjoy.' He paused and gave me a knowing smile, which did nothing to ease my chagrin. 'Your rooms are adjoining. Please feel at liberty to make your own arrangements as you wish. As I said, you are free now. You may do as you choose.' I knew exactly what he meant, and judging from the red tide which swept up Jane's pretty face, so did she.

Sir Gordon called at the palace later in the day and made the same speech, with slightly less directness, that he had made to me about us finding a safe haven – a kind of 'retreat' to accustom ourselves to our liberty. When we were alone again, I told my companions, my voice pained, about the video the president had shown me in the ambassador's presence, and their insistence about the necessity of remaining silent, or at least disguising the truth about our ordeal. Hence, Jack's fierce outburst.

'They can't keep us hidden away, or shut up, for ever,' he ranted on indignantly. 'I tell you; there's a fortune to be made out there. It's waiting, worldwide. Our story; the way it really is and has been. We could tell the whole world Koloba's real role with those kidnapping bastards, and the deals that must have been struck between them. We could tell the whole world!' he repeated fervently.

I glared at him, my hands at my sides clenched into tight fists. 'For God's sake, Jack!' I exclaimed. 'Do you really want to tell the truth?' I gestured at all four of us. 'Shall I ask the president to let you see the tape? I've told you, it's all there! Every sordid detail of what we got up to! Carl and Me in the shower! Jane and you… all of us… *together!* Is that what you want the world to know about?' The other two looked as sickened and ashamed as I felt, but Jack's expression looked positively ugly, his face twisted in a beleaguered defiance.

'So what?' he snorted. 'We can always say they forced us into it. In fact they *did* force us into it, didn't they? We would never normally have done everything we did, not exactly. That's what comes from running around naked for months like animals in a cage, which is how they kept us. That certainly wasn't our doing.'

'Oh yeah, you can see on the tape just how reluctant you were to screw Jane!' I countered vehemently. 'You were clearly forced so much to behave in an unaccustomed way and so reluctant to participate that it's amazing you ever got it up!' I felt a stab of guilt when I heard Jane's sob of pain and shame, but I could not help myself. I was sick with rage at Jack's attitude. Why couldn't he just be thankful we had emerged from the whole rotten business safely? Why did he keep insisting on making trouble for us?

He stared coldly at me. 'And you, babe,' he said, his tone level and cutting. 'I don't see any scratches on Koloba's face where you tried to fight him off.'

'Stop it!' Jane suddenly cried. 'Both of you, stop it! All this bickering is going to do us no good at all!'

'Oh yes,' I snarled spitefully, ignoring Jane's sensible plea for calm; I was suddenly filled with a raging fury for what we had been put through, and I aimed all my suppressed feelings at Jack, whose belligerent attitude was making him a simple and obvious target, 'the president *does* bear scratches, and other marks of passion too, but you won't get to see them.' Jack fell silent and just stared at me, but I wanted to go on; I wanted to hurt him. 'They're on his back, you see. I got so carried away at the way he made me orgasm so wonderfully and so easily and so frequently...'

Jack just stared at me, his shoulders sagging, and I

instantly loathed myself and wished I could take such bitchy words back. But it was too late, they had been said, and they hung ominously in the air between us.

'I don't really want to interrupt your little tiff, but I'd just like to remind you all that we're not actually free yet, no matter how well they appear to be treating us.' Carl's quiet voice was in such contrast to the raw emotion simmering between Jack and me that it pulled us up short and introduced an air of reason into the room.

'What's the alternative if we don't go along with what they want?' he continued, once he saw that he had defused the confrontation between the two of us and had our attention. 'What is the alternative,' he repeated, 'for the present, at least? And don't forget the press conference is arranged for tomorrow. Right here, in the palace of our brave liberator. And those security guys from our embassy will be there.' He looked at each of us in turn, clearly surprised by our lack of reaction. 'Did you not notice them?' he asked. 'Particularly dangerous individuals, if you ask me, and not the sort we should consider getting on the wrong side of. They were some extremely fit looking specimens for trade attachés, wouldn't you say? I'll tell you now – I for one will be saying exactly what Sir Gordon tells me to say. And I'd advise you lot to do the same, if you ever want to get out of here in one piece.'

Chapter Twenty

In the end we all heeded Carl's advice, though Jack muttered privately how different things would be 'once we get the hell out of this dump'. I thought it was somewhat unfair to describe our present surroundings as a 'dump'; our rooms were part of the sumptuous guest wing of the presidential palace. We each had a whole new wardrobe of designer labelled clothing to choose from, first class food, and a retinue of servants to attend to our every hedonistic wish. So, it was not surprising that the world media should assume from our well groomed appearance that we had received nothing but generous treatment at the hands of the president during all the long months of our captivity. And, despite my intense anxiety, none of us, including my husband, gave them cause to think anything else.

Mind you, the media's presence at the conference had been carefully controlled. There were television cameras there and news agency representatives, but not that many. The Leontondese authorities, quietly and ably assisted by British government officials, who kept a very low profile, screened most of the footage that went out to the world about us.

A very low profile, I should say, all except Sir Gordon, who was very much out front fielding and filtering all the questions, smoothing over any awkward moments, such as the question which came from one of the foreign journalists who referred to the testimony of Nicky Gimburg, which seemed to suggest that the use of physical and sexual abuse had taken place on a disturbing level.

Sir Gordon jumped in swiftly. 'Well, these good people cannot speak for what might or might not have happened privately outside their presence. I seem to remember several of the hostages confirmed that even on the plane there were altercations between Ms Gimburg and the hijackers. As Mr and Mrs Freeman and Mr and Mrs Kinsella have been at pains to stress, once the distressing early stages of their confinement passed and the four of them were reunited, thanks to the good auspices of President Koloba as well as our own quietly unceasing efforts on their behalf, they have been treated extremely well.

'As I am sure you will all agree, ladies and gentlemen, from their remarkably reassuring appearance here today before you after the trauma of their long spell under duress, that point is clearly confirmed.'

However, even the suave diplomat was clearly relieved when the conference was drawn to a close, after we had posed for a final picture, grouped around the beaming president, his arms draped heavily round Jane and me, resting on our shoulders, while our spouses' arms snaked in righteous possession about our waists.

As soon as we had left the room Jack sought out Sir Gordon, his features set in a determined scowl. 'That was a load of rubbish!' he said aggressively. 'A complete farce, and you can't expect us to keep it up just to make you look good. I don't care what you've got on tape. I don't give a damn! We've a right to let people know what really happened to us, what we've been through. Call it compensation, if you like. But there's a lot of folk who will pay good money – very good money – to hear what really happened to us!'

Sir Gordon stood and took the outburst and never batted an eyelid. Keeping his voice low and controlled, he answered, 'Yes, of course, I'm sure you're right. But have you considered how it will affect you, what public opinion will be, if all the truth comes out? Have you considered how all four of you adjusted to life at the compound? I am referring of course to your sexual activities. The people out there may feel you are totally unreliable once they are aware of what went on. They may – and believe me, they probably will – feel that anything you say is not to be trusted. And the media moguls may not feel like parting with their money for what their readers and viewers and listeners regard as nothing but an unreliable pack of lies.'

He put his arm round Jack's shoulder, steering him, and us, away from prying ears and eyes, smiling that urbane smile of his all the while, as though he was merely chatting about the weather or the latest cricket scores. 'But, on the matter of compensation, I think you will find our government can be most sympathetic – and generous – when it comes to repaying you for the torment you have endured and for your cooperation and discretion in what is a difficult and stressful situation for all concerned.'

'Buy our silence, you mean?' Jack said, and Jane and I blushed at his bluntness. 'Well, we don't come cheap, I can tell you that for nothing.'

'I'm sure you do not,' Sir Gordon said smoothly, and smiled with infuriating confidence. 'And I am sure your worth will not be underestimated.' He turned away as Koloba and his senior aides came over to us.

'Ah, Mr President,' he said warmly, as though the conversation just concluded had never taken place, 'it all went off rather well, don't you think? And our friends played their part admirably, I must say.'

The president's booming laugh rolled out over us in a veritable wave of unrestrained mirth, and I felt my toes squirming under the directness of his gaze. 'Yes indeed, Sir Gordon,' he chortled cheerfully. 'Anyone would think they had been coached on their lines...'

We remained a further week at the palace, troubled no longer by journalists or any other outside influence. We were treated as VIP's, taken around the country's game parks and all the other tourist attractions we had never gotten to know during our long months of confinement. Our main mode of transport was the helicopter, the very machine in which Koloba had screwed me. I felt uncomfortable being in it with Jack, who was totally oblivious to what had taken place over the very seat on which he sat beside me.

I also felt uncomfortable at Kamau's polite greeting, unable to forget the bizarre circumstances of our first meeting, but apart from a fleeting and surreptitious smile and glance at Jack, that my husband fortunately did not notice, he made no references, veiled or otherwise, to the shameful incident, and I soon relaxed.

In fact, I became more embarrassed and uncomfortable

at the sudden emotional strains that seemed to have sprung up between the four of us. We struggled to be determinedly jolly, and to ignore the peculiar links that had forged our special relationship. At night, in our luxurious bedroom, Jack made love to me with his accustomed fervour, and I responded in kind, though once the frolicking and fucking were done we had little to say to each other.

Chapter Twenty-One

It was inevitable, I suppose, that the three of us accepted Jack as the leader of our quartet as his dominating personality came more and more to the fore. We never discussed it, nor did we show any sign of objecting; it was just a natural development. We were weary and he was bullish and aggressive, so it just happened. Jane and I – and Carl, we were increasingly realising – had always had that willingness to be subservient in our sex play, but this was different, something much deeper and more fundamental. The long months of our captivity had brought about profound changes in us. It had brought out those facets of our personalities that had either lain dormant or that we had kept decently suppressed up until that watershed in our lives. Whatever the reason, Jack assumed a responsibility for us that extended beyond the games we played in the bedroom or bathroom.

And others clearly recognised it too, particularly Sir Gordon, who soon looked to Jack as our spokesman and decision maker, virtually ignoring the thoughts and opinions of we other three.

'We have found an ideal place for you to recuperate,' the diplomat told us, on one of his almost daily visits. 'It is a beautiful tropical isle, no less. Have any of you ever heard of Lord Staith?'

We all looked suitably mystified, and so Sir Gordon went

on to explain.

'I am not surprised that you have not,' he said, relaxed in our company but always somewhat formal, determined to remain in control of a potentially explosive situation. 'Lord Staith keeps a deliberate low profile, but he is one of the most powerful and influential figures around – both in the UK and on the world scene at large. He is fabulously wealthy and has a finger in most pies.

'Well, it is his island that we are proposing to send you to for a while. It is called Kendu, in the Indian Ocean off the East African coast. It is absolutely ideal for our purposes. It is only about an hour's helicopter flight from here, and Lord Staith has very kindly put it at our disposal for as long as we want it. You will be able to indulge in sun, sea and sand, and you will live in the lap of luxury during your whole stay. Who could ask for anything more?'

He was trying to tell us something, I thought, behind that urbane manner of his.

And Jack was quick to pick up on it as well. 'And how long are we going to be kept on this island paradise?' Before Sir Gordon could answer him he went on. 'Do we have any choice in the matter,' he pressed, 'or are we being effectively kidnapped again – but this time by our own people? I'm pretty sure I speak for the others,' he nodded at Carl and Jane, 'but I can safely say that Moira and me wouldn't mind getting back to England – getting back home. We've been taken out of civilisation for the past year, and now we should be allowed to get our lives back. And you owe us that. We've got a lot of catching up to do.'

Sir Gordon looked indignant, and a little flustered, clearly reading Jack's thinly veiled accusation. 'But there is no rush, is there?' he asked, without too much conviction. 'Why not make the most of such a generous opportunity? Believe me, there are not many people who ever get the sort of a chance you are being given, and most people would have to pay a fortune to enjoy a luxury holiday that still would not even compare to what we are offering you.

'And besides the enviable time you will have in paradise,' the ambassador went on, recovering his aplomb very nicely, 'Lord Staith can prove tremendously helpful, whatever you choose to do. As I said, there is not much he has not got control over... including the media,' he added significantly. 'At least give Kendu a few weeks? I assure you, it can only do you good – give you a chance to recharge your batteries.'

Then something happened that gave us further cause for serious thought. In our quieter moments, which were increasingly numerous, Jane and I had speculated a great deal about what had happened to our fellow hostages, especially Nicky and Anita, to whom we had grown closest in those early days of captivity.

But we found it oddly difficult to gain any hard news or facts about either of them. We were fobbed off when we asked if we could see the reaction in the press to their release, which had taken place more than six months before.

Then for no apparent reason the redoubtable Sir Gordon became much more cooperative on the matter. One morning he showed up with a box full of material.

'I had hoped to spare you this,' he declared ominously. 'It is very recent, as you will see from the dates of the press cuttings.'

The first we looked at was only two weeks old:

EX-HOSTAGE DISAPPEARS. BODY FOUND ON MONTANA RANCH

Police are anxious to trace the whereabouts of twenty-year-old Nicky Gimburg, who last year was a passenger on an aeroplane hijacked by terrorists and held prisoner in Leontondo. After her release, she gave a lurid account of punishments and sexual abuse, particularly by the female member of the kidnap gang, German born Krista Wiel. Nicky, a student, and athlete of considerable promise, took up a reclusive life on a spread in a remote area of Montana, with her partner and lesbian lover, thirty-six-year-old Donna Steiner.

Two days ago, a hired hand discovered the naked and beaten body of Ms Steiner in the bedroom she shared with Ms Gimburg. There was no trace of her younger partner, and none of Ms Gimburg's clothing or personal possessions were left at the ranch. The hand who made the discovery, forty-three-year-old Kevin Marks, told police that a dark-haired young woman had arrived at the ranch three days ago, and had apparently stayed there overnight.

The next day, Mr Marks had seen her vehicle leaving the property. The stranger, who was driving, was accompanied by Ms Gimburg. The following morning, when neither Ms Steiner nor Ms Gimburg had appeared as they usually did, he went up to the ranch-house for instructions, and after a brief search he discovered the body of Ms Steiner in the main bedroom.

There were other clippings, all from American papers, but adding nothing of any further help. Jane was crying quietly. 'She wasn't... she wasn't a lesbian,' she murmured, sadly shaking her head. 'Not until Krista...' her voice faded.

I cleared my throat. 'What are they saying?' I pondered aloud. 'That Nicky was implicated in the killing? They think she and this other woman murdered her partner?'

Sir Gordon hesitated, looking uncomfortable in the face of our sadness. 'There is something else,' he said at last, 'something that has not been made public. But our anti-terrorist chaps got hold of it, and they think it might be relevant – in your situation.' He passed over a large, rather grainy black and white photograph, which had clearly been enlarged several times. 'They think this might be the mystery visitor that turned up at the ranch.'

There was a head and shoulders image of a pretty, dark-haired young woman, her features rendered largely anonymous by the sunglasses that blanked out her eyes. Although she was facing the camera, she did not look as though she was posing for the picture. In fact, it looked as though she was not aware of it being taken.

We stared at it for long minutes, at a loss, and then glanced up enquiringly at Sir Gordon.

'Try to blot out the sunglasses,' he suggested, 'and the dark hair. Imagine blue eyes... and short, very blonde hair.' He put the tip of his forefinger over the top of her head. 'Look very, very carefully at that face…'

My heart hammered and I gave a small gasp that was simultaneously echoed by Jane. We stared, appalled. 'Krista!' we breathed together.

Sir Gordon nodded. 'In our opinion, the sooner we get you away from here, the better.' He shrugged. 'If our fears are justified and somehow she got hold of that girl again…

'We do not know anything else about the whereabouts or safety of Ms Gimburg, I am afraid. But I would feel far happier if you were on Kendu, where we could guarantee your safety. And so would you if you have got any sense whatsoever.'

'Hi, my name's Sas. I'll be looking after you while you're here. Anything you want at all, or if there's anything wrong, you just let me know. His lordship will be here in a couple of days, and I know he's looking forward very much to meeting you all.'

We were all staring open-mouthed at the beautiful creature who stood smiling before us. She was entirely naked. Her body was a deep toasted brown all over, with no sign of white flashes even at her full breasts, whose dark nipples stood out in ripe magnificence, or beneath the tuft of pubic curls which glinted in sun-bleached paleness to match her straight, simply cut blonde hair.

The swirl of hot air and the blast of fine blown sand brought us back to our senses as the small helicopter lifted from the level stretch of short coarse grass above the dazzling white beach, and headed off, dark against the sun, back to the distant mainland.

But our gaze was drawn again to the captivating vision of the girl, and now to her pertly rolling buttocks in particular as she led the way to a huddled group of squat, grass-roofed buildings, the modest exteriors of which belied the luxury inside. She was not apparently in the least bit embarrassed by our presence or gawping expressions, or by the grinning porters who were carrying our luggage, and whose modesty was assured by the khaki shorts they wore.

And another surprise awaited us on the low veranda of smoothly polished concrete. There was another naked figure, a slim young man this time, whose hair, both on his scalp and at the base of his flat belly, though a lot darker than Sas's, had the same sun-kissed appearance to fit with the deep mahogany tan of his skin.

But it was not all this that gripped my attention. No, it was his paler penis hanging down between his thighs, a good five inches at least in length though it was perfectly flaccid. And at the tip of its helmet, which was completely exposed, was affixed a gleaming ring of silver metal.

'This is Pete,' Sas told us cheerfully. 'He'll also help to make your stay as comfortable and pleasurable as possible. He's available for anything you need, at all times, ladies,' she said, her tone heavily laden with inference. 'And I mean *anything*.'

I giggled like a teenager, but managed to wrench my gaze away from that impressive penis as he held out his hand. Like the girl, his brown eyes showed no trace of embarrassment at his nakedness.

'That's right, ladies,' he said, smiling confidently, 'if

there's any way I can serve you, don't hesitate to ask.'

I giggled again rather foolishly, my mind already running riot.

'And does that go for you too, Sas?' Jack asked. 'Are *you* available for anything we need, at all times?'

The lovely girl stared levelly at him, her look implying it was a silly question. 'Of course it does, Mr Kinsella,' she said. 'Or do you mind if I call you Jack? I'd like it if we could be on first name terms from the outset.' She moved closer to him as she spoke, so that those lovely breasts of hers were practically grazing his arm, and knowing my husband like I did, I could almost hear his cock straining to get out of his trousers.

And it wasn't long before it made its escape. 'When in Rome,' Jack crowed happily a few minutes later, when we had surveyed our new quarters. The buildings were a series of bungalows; all fitted out with wonderfully furnished accommodations, including tiled toilets and bathrooms, in spite of the primitive, unspoilt surroundings. He was already throwing off his clothes, and we did the same at once.

There was a long communal dining area on the edge of the beach, with paved flooring and without walls, its grass roof supported on stout wooden pillars. The local natives, of a pleasing golden brown complexion, paler than the darker skinned inhabitants of the mainland, supplied the plentiful domestic staff.

And despite the length of time we had gone unclothed during our captivity, I found myself attacked by an awkward shyness, and I could see Jane was feeling the same way as the smiling natives gazed frankly at us. The slender men all wore cheap colourful sarongs or shorts, and the girls wore sarongs too, which dipped at the front to allow the graceful little pout of their bellies to show. They were bare breasted, and that helped Jane and I to feel a little better. It seemed strange, though, that only the white folk went completely naked here. However, there was a lot that was strange in our new environment, as we were to learn very soon, over the next few days.

After a long and excellently cooked and served lunch, washed down with small bottles of iced French beer, Jack rose without preamble and reached for Sas's hand; she and Peter had eaten with us. It was clear that they were recognised by the servants as superiors, and seemed to be in overall charge while Lord Staith was away. 'Let's make a start on getting better acquainted,' Jack said to Sas, smiling broadly.

I coloured uncomfortably at his bluntness, and was annoyed that he seemed to think, probably because of all we had been through and done together, that it was now okay to be promiscuous – or selfish, as I considered it – without consulting or considering me or my feelings. It also put Carl and Jane in an awkward position, but the experience we had all been through seemed to have changed Jack more than we three… and not necessarily changed him for the better, I might add.

But without hesitation, Sas rose with alluring nubile grace, letting him lead her back up the short sloping beaten track, through the tall coconut palms, towards our designated bungalow.

Jack then turned at the top of the track, and called back to our male host. 'Help yourself, Peter. Feel free to entertain them as you like.' He nodded carelessly at the three of us trying to relax on the low sun-loungers, and my blood boiled. An angry retort sprang to mind, but it did not pass my lips. One thing I had learned during my long stint as a hostage and a sex slave was self-control.

Peter was smiling, looking at us politely, waiting, and in a daredevil mood that was part defiance at Jack's careless proprietorship, I got up off the lounger. 'Yes, I think I'd like you to "entertain" me a little, Peter,' I said daringly. Well, if it was good for Jack, it was good for me! 'And why don't you and Carl come along?' I said to Jane, but she just looked back at me, her brown eyes wide and troubled as she tried to shade them from the sun with her hand.

Peter stepped smoothly into the moment of awkwardness. 'Come on,' he urged Jane warmly, 'it'll be fun.' Then smiling with undeniable charm he offered his hand, and Jane reached up to take it, letting him lift her up from the recliner. His invitation was also extended to the silent Carl, and all four of us headed up the track – not, I observed with satisfaction, to our bungalow, where Jack had taken Sas, but to an identical one across the sparse, cropped lawn.

And Peter was right; it *did* turn out to be fun – immense fun – and certainly different. Peter proved to be an accomplished lover; an ability he ably demonstrated several times to both Jane and me during the hot, passionate hours of the afternoon, which did not exclude Carl, despite the noticeable contrast between his average penis and Peter's lusty member. For the moment Jack was forgotten, and the sun had long disappeared into the ocean before exhaustion brought our fun to an end.

'Ohhh…' I groaned when Peter had departed and Carl, Jane and I were lying in companionable weariness in a bath full of fragrant foam. 'What a way to go! I am well and truly shattered!'

So it was not really surprising that, after a wonderful dinner, we lay under the stars – Jack had rejoined us by then – too pleasantly worn out to do anything except talk idly and drink exotic cocktails. Sas and Peter told us some more about our host, which only added to our intrigue, and nervousness, at the prospect of our imminent introduction to him.

'He's a fine master,' Sas declared easily, though I'm sure she was well aware of the verbal bombshell she had tossed with that last word. We echoed it in astonishment, and she gave a seductively musical chuckle. 'Oh yes indeed, we belong to him,' she confirmed mischievously, 'don't we, Peter?

'That's exactly what he is,' she went on without awaiting his response, 'our master. And you'll find he has a number of others like us. He owns us all. We're his slaves, you see.'

At that moment, hearing her innocently silky voice declare such things, and gazing upon the equally innocently beautiful visage from whence the words came, I felt my naked body tremble from head to toe. It was a shiver of… what, exactly? Was it fear? Yes, I think it certainly was. But it was something else too; something deep, a purely instinctive reaction, a frisson of excitement, of something lodged deep inside my core.

Chapter Twenty-Two

'I think his lordship would rather see you as nature intended, babe. After all, you've got nothing to be ashamed of. Has she, Sas?'

My eyes widened at Jack's careless words, and I gazed at the steady features of the lovely girl as she agreed wholeheartedly with him. He had spent most of the three days we had been on Kendu closeted away with her, and already there was an exclusive intimacy between them that stung me with a combined sense of resentment, jealously, and injustice. But then there would be, I thought, because he was my husband and he was effectively being unfaithful to me right under my nose, and somehow using our predicament and what we'd been through as justification for his behaviour. At least, he was justifying it to himself, if not to the rest of us.

Her sparkling blue eyes slid away from mine diplomatically, and I knew she was well aware of what was going through my turbulent mind.

'You too, Jane,' Jack said, with that beaming grin of his which did not disguise the baldness of what was clearly an order.

Jane blushed, but to my discomfort she reached back and groped for the zip fastener on the flowered sundress she was wearing. Carefully she removed the garment, easing it from her breasts, which were already acquiring a pale creamy tan. The white triangle of her thong briefs just covered her mound, and I could see the misty shadow of her pubic hair through the fine material.

Her thumbs hooked into the bootlace-thin straps at her hips and slipped the tiny cover down her shapely legs. They tangled in the light sandals, which she also slipped off as she flipped the knickers off her feet. 'Is that better?' she asked uncertainly, yet she had not even hesitated to carry out his command. What on earth, I wondered, was happening to us? I hurried to strip off the dress and knickers I had chosen with such care only minutes ago to meet Lord Staith for the first time.

'What about Carl?' I asked maliciously, and immediately regretted my wickedness, especially when Jack glanced across at the silent figure, who was wearing a smart, short sleeved shirt and white linen slacks. My husband's wolfish smile broadened.

'Sure. Come on, buddy boy. Get your kit off and let's feast our eyes on that cute little todger of yours.' I choked back my protest as Carl swiftly divested himself of what little clothing he had on and came and stood close to Jane and me. 'That's better. Let's go.' Jack slapped playfully at my behind, and Jane's, and then threw his arms about our shoulders and led us into the blazing sunshine, and down onto the hot white sand. The planks of the short jetty were equally hot beneath our bare feet as we stood nervously and watched the dazzling white hull of the yacht approach.

Any discomfort or embarrassment was quickly forgotten as we gazed open-mouthed at the spectacle that presented itself. As the elegant vessel nosed alongside, we saw that its crew consisted of five beautiful white girls, all as naked as we were. Except that they weren't white, but a subtle variety of richly tanned shades as comprehensive as that of the lovely Sas, and equally entrancing to behold. They skipped lithely about the deck, and two leapt ashore over the narrow gap between the boat's side and the quay and made fast the mooring ropes. The only male member of the crew appeared to be the grizzled face we could see at the window of the neat bridge, who nodded with curt satisfaction at the able performance of his exotic subordinates.

With the boat safely docked, all five girls sprang ashore and stood in line, like a guard of honour, all smartly at attention, arms rigidly at their sides, eyes staring straight ahead. My gaze travelled with rapid appreciation over their differing but attractive proportions. Then I stared in fascination as the sun sent a twinkling, identical sparkle from the neat tufts of pubic hair, and I saw five small silver rings fixed through the upper folds of their labia. I was still gawping when I heard a rich, plummy chuckle and our host came into sight and stepped over the short gangplank.

What first struck me about this legendary figure was the boyish twinkle of mischief in the grey eyes, the exuberant, roly-poly joy of life he exuded. There was an air of innocence about him, a childlike enthusiasm which belied his obviously mature years. His ruddy features were plain and rounded, his grey hair was cut extremely short, and so thin on top that the pink of his scalp showed through. But his skin was smooth, fragrant, witness to the extensive grooming it habitually received from the elite corps of retainers he took around the world with him. He was short, only a couple of inches taller than me, and plump. He made no effort to hide his less than athletic shape. Rather, he seemed to derive much pleasure from it. His belly thrust out like a woman in an advanced stage of pregnancy, contrasting with the small daintiness of his limbs, his perfectly tended hands and feet.

And it was all on show for, beneath an ornate cloak slung loosely over his shoulders, held at the front by a gold chain and clasp, and reaching down at the back to just below his chubby buttocks, he wore nothing but a pouch, just fitted snugly over his genitals – a tiny cache-sexe of the softest leather and studded with sparkling points of light we discovered later really were diamonds. A black string at his hips secured this miniscule cover over his penis and testicles, joined by another at the back that hid deep in the crack of his backside. The cloak was a rich reddish brown colour, with intricate designs sewn into it. We learnt that it was woven by the islanders, and was the symbol of his authority as a paramount chief over them. Apart from these two items, the only other clothing he wore was a simple, very cheap pair of rubber thonged sandals, flip-flops you could buy at any street stall for a few cents.

The twinkling gaze passed over Jane and me like a caress I could almost feel. He came towards us with outstretched arms and hugged us to his body. His belly was like a tight drum against me. His hands slid down, clutched at my bottom, massaging each cheek with cosy intimacy. His lips brushed mine and his tongue flickered swiftly between my teeth and was gone again just as quickly.

'Delighted to meet you at last!' that rich voice welcomed us, with apparently sincere warmth. He turned to Jack and gripped his hand firmly. 'Your girls are absolutely exquisite,' he beamed, and my gaze flicked over to Jane in silent comment at our relegation to collective ownership.

'Oh, I say!' Another of his deep chuckles diverted my thoughts. His lordship was staring delightedly at the white figure of Carl, who for once looked a little discomfited. His hands twitched, and I thought for one second he was going to close them over that sweet cock of his, but they clenched into fists, and he kept them stiffly at his sides, rather like the female boat crew still standing waiting to be dismissed.

I was nonplussed. We all adjourned to the open dining area and began a splendid lunch in what seemed to be jolly camaraderie at the long table, with his lordship at its head, Sas and Peter, ourselves, the naked girls from the boat, and the male skipper and engineer. Yet it was clear from the first that Staith considered Jane, Carl and me, as subservient to Jack. I wanted to say something, to speak out, to correct him of this misconception, yet some instinct warned me to keep quiet. Not here, I reassured myself, accustomed to keeping silent and doing what I was told to avoid potentially unpleasant repercussions. And this place was a whole new enigma. Everything seemed nice enough on the surface, but I had learned to mistrust appearances. So I held my tongue. I would not confront Jack about his behaviour yet, not yet, not in public like this. But later, in private, I would let my husband know in no uncertain terms that we would not be treated like this.

I felt tense, even a little faint and sick inside, despite the splendid food and copious amounts of drink. I found I was keeping silent, responding only to the questions directed at me, letting Jack do all the talking for us as though he really did own us. And Jane was no better. She was letting him get away with it, too. He was like some cocky pimp and we were his girls, helpless to do anything about our situation.

And then I discovered that I had drunk a lot more wine than I realised. Without warning, I could feel my face glowing and my head spinning, and it added unpleasantly to the slightly nauseous sensation in my stomach. So I reached across and tapped Jane's arm. 'I need to go to the bathroom,' I whispered. 'Come with me.'

But as we rose, somewhat unsteadily, Staith glanced up with that beneficent, rosy smile. 'Girls, take Moira and Jane over to your quarters,' he said to his collection of attentive beauties. 'Have a good old chat. Get to know each other a little better, and we'll see you later.'

We had been dismissed, I thought haughtily, but found myself being led away, surrounded by all that lovely female flesh, with much giggling and bumping of hips against hips and breasts against arms. The girls took us to a building right at the edge of the beach.

'I – I wasn't joking back there,' I said. 'I must have a pee. I'm bursting. I – I need a pee before I have an accident.'

'And you're not the only one,' giggled one of the girls, 'so do I!' And amidst chirpy laughter, we were hustled to the bathroom, and then stopped, staring in wonder from the doorway. There was a row of lavatory pedestals along one wall, and along another a row of bidets. Several washbasins, in the same pristinely shining porcelain, stood in snug neighbourliness under the wide expanse of a mirror. At the other side of the room were three bathtubs, then a tiled recess with a row of showers. And, most significantly, all this had been built with not one compartment or dividing screen between any of the sanitary facilities.

Mags, who was apparently the senior member of this unique crew, made straight for the nearest toilet and sat down upon it, with an inviting wave. 'Come on, help yourself,' she beckoned, and then sighed blissfully, and I heard the strong hiss as she urinated. She was the tallest and most statuesque of all the girls. Her breasts were full, ripe with promise, and her shoulders square, the muscles outlined on her arms and her firm thighs in a way that reminded me of Nicky. I paused, glanced helplessly round at Jane, but then realised I was now in dire need to relieve myself. Beggars could not be choosers, so I hastily sat on the lavatory next to Mags, and thankfully did just that. In a second Jane was next to me, and then all seats were occupied as we squatted companionably.

The bedroom was equally communal. Five low futons were spaced around the walls, and there was a long shelf, with a mirror above it and cushioned stools beneath it, which served as a common dressing table and was covered with an assortment of cosmetics.

Mags told us briefly something of their history, without filling in too many details at all. 'We were all together before,' she explained. 'We were in the navy. Then Lord Staith got hold of us; it was a sort of pressgang in reverse.

That was quite some time ago. Now we're all happy little galley slaves aboard the *Lady Jane*.' She laughed breezily. 'Yes, that really is its name. And quite appropriate too, wouldn't you say?'

A willowy girl with tight blonde curls and a languid accent which indicated a privileged background, asked Jane and I conversationally and totally out of the blue, 'So what's your man like? He looks pretty dishy to me, I must say, but is he good to you or is he a bastard?'

The frankness of the strange questions took the two of us so much by surprise that we stared open-mouthed at her. So the blonde, whose name was Beth, merely raised an amused eyebrow. 'Oh come on now, you can trust us,' she went on. 'We won't breathe a word, honestly. Give us all the details. He'll probably want one or more of us tonight,' she sniggered lewdly, 'so any kinky little habits we should know about?

'I say,' she went on, leaning closer and looking around conspiratorially, 'he's not into other men, is he? After all, the other one looks a bit sweet. Where does he fit in?' she giggled. 'If you'll pardon the expression!'

'Jack's my husband!' I hastily exclaimed, trying to hide my amusement at what the girl had said about him behind a mask of indignation, instinctively feeling I should defend my husband, but then quickly wondering why I should considering the way he had been behaving lately. 'He's not *our* man.'

'And the "sweet" one is mine,' Jane added. 'My husband, I mean.'

'Oh,' said Mags, and then indicated our state of nakedness with a confused expression. 'But surely you belong to Lord Staith now?'

The word 'belong' rang round and round in my reeling brain. Even as a denial sprang indignantly to my lips, the shadow of such a shocking possibility seemed to cloud my mind. I shook my head and sank down on the nearest free mattress.

'Belong?' I echoed wearily. 'We don't *belong* to anybody. We'll be leaving here soon, and going home...'

Suddenly a new feeling, or rather, a nagging and overpoweringly familiar feeling, took over. The girls had closed in on us.

I felt firm but gentle hands rubbing my ankles and arms, pressing me back and down into the softness beneath me. Then the hands crept up, caressing my shins and calves and thighs, others cupped my tingling breasts and stroking my neck and shoulders.

The girls loomed over me, their silky flesh pressing more and more intimately against me, smothering me with their fragrant beauty.

Lips possessed mine and a warm wet mouth kissed my breast, its tongue flickering over my engorged nipple, while another gave the same adoration to its twin. The mouths opened, suckled greedily, and I moaned, let myself go, yielding willingly to the hands that were opening me up, exploring that wet and demanding cleft between my thighs, drawing out every particle of delightful excitement from its running centre, stretching me on the sweetly merciless rack of desire.

My body turned, writhed, and I sobbed in helpless need. 'Don't stop... don't stop...' I heard myself begging and somehow, somewhere in my fragmenting mind, I knew that Jane was with me, as we both plunged and flowed on the rising tide of passion that swamped us.

'I recommend this at least once a day for the first month. And a proper whipping too – we're not talking love taps here. The little fillies come to love it, believe me. It lets them know you're their master. And that's what they want more than anything in the world. Isn't it, my sweet little Moira?'

I could not see him. My head and wrists were firmly clamped in the circular holes of the wooden stocks. A horizontal bar, also constructed of wood, pressed up firmly across my lower belly, nestling uncomfortably against my pubic bone. It ensured that my body, from the hips upward, was bent at right angles to my widely parted legs, my ankles shackled to the two upright supporters of the whole frame.

Alongside me, though I could not see them either, Jane and Carl were similarly pinioned. Thus, our three bottoms were proffered in the bathing sunshine for the punishment about to be inflicted upon them.

Lord Staith's words were spoken close by my side. I could feel his warm breath on my shoulder, and I felt his hands stroking my breasts as they hung naked, teasing them until my nipples ached and stood out in rubbery hardness.

Then he let one hand slide slowly down my belly, until he was plucking at the silky tendrils of my pubes. I bit my lip, gasping with renewed hunger when his fingers traced the damp lips of my cunt, sending it throbbing to heightened arousal. My thigh muscles locked, my haunches tightened, and I whimpered at this stimulation, feeling the sticky wetness seep over the probing fingertips. I tried to push my belly forward and down a little, to increase the pressure of those taunting fingers, but the hardness of the wood thrust unyieldingly back against my pelvis and I moaned with frustration.

'There, there, my dear,' the aristocratic tones purred, the fingers sending the fires of desire ever stronger through my captive flesh. 'You'll soon feel something far more delicious eating away at you, and you'll express your gratitude to your master, won't you?'

Master, he said it again. I shook, and a huge sob wracked my bound body. Jack was not, I wanted to shriek, my master! I was nobody's slave! But then, what was I doing there, in the burning tropic sun, naked and tethered like some sacrifice and about to be whipped like a dumb beast, with all the other naked figures and a considerable crowd of excited villagers watching avidly? And the man who was going to wield the whip, that sleek instrument of chastisement we had already been introduced to, was undoubtedly at that moment entitled to the term 'master'.

Lord Staith let the three long lashes trail softly over our bare backs. 'See these strands?' he asked, addressing Jack, for our position clearly meant we could not. 'Bound in silk, they are. You can lay them on as hard as you like, and they won't cut the skin or scar it permanently in any way.

'And you must lay it on as hard as you can,' his lordship urged Jack, and for the first time his voice thickened, betraying the excitement that was making his squat penis stir and thrust against the soft chamois nest that closeted it. 'It is essential that you do so,' he continued earnestly. 'They must be absolutely certain that you are their lord and master. They must be left in no doubt that they belong to you.' His voice lightened again. 'And that applies even to Carl!'

'Don't worry, your lordship; they'll know who is their boss all right!' Jack's voice was also hoarse with excitement. And perhaps a little uncertainty too, I speculated. For all his bravado, this was a situation as novel to him as it was to us. In his own way he was facing a test, just as we were.

But he was as good as his word. I was the first in line. There was the briefest of whistling sounds as the air was disturbed that I felt as much as heard as the triple lash descended. With a sharp crack a ripple of fire bit through my clenched cheeks, and the wooden frame shook and creaked as I fought desperately against my restraints. In an additional fine flare of agony the tips of the lashes curled around my hip and bit into the crease of my belly and thigh. The wooden rings cosseting my neck and wrists chafed as I twisted, and the iron rubbed my ankles as I strove to move, to kick out, but they went unnoticed in the world of throbbing torment covering my bottom.

I've no idea how long I waited, sobbing blindly, for the next strike. Only that it seemed an age, as Jack moved along the line punishing all three in turn, one stroke for each, before returning to deliver the second to my still scorching bottom.

The lashes swept down again and I went through the same howling dance of ordeal. My poor bottom felt as though the skin was split, though when later I saw the results of the beating on my own flesh and that of Jane and Carl, I had to admit that his lordship's words had been correct. Though our behinds and the backs of our thighs were covered in a profusion of thin, lividly red raised weals, not one millimetre of our skin was broken. And though the weals remained visible for days, darkening to a rich multi-hue of bruising, continuing to ache abominably and to be overlaid with the fresh marks of the subsequent beatings we endured, eventually they faded and disappeared, leaving our skin as smoothly unblemished as it had been before.

My world had shrunk to a blazing torment of agonised flesh, but then, with a shock that soared perversely over that private universe of pain, I felt a glow of consuming arousal, infinitely more powerful than the excitement caused on my captured body by Staith's inquisitive fingers. It seemed to flow along with the pain, I felt myself running with it, my sex pulsing deliciously in climax. My muscles locked, every part of me fused to this sensation, my legs were rigid as iron as I tensed and lifted my mortified flesh to that consuming fire. I was opened to the very core of my being.

From far away, through my waves of ecstasy and confusion, I heard Jack's voice demanding, 'Who is your master?'

'You are!' I instantly blabbered without thinking twice. 'You are my master!'

Some time later I returned vaguely to awareness of my surroundings, and the pain, which wrapped itself like a hot blanket around my flesh. Fingers were probing urgently between my thighs, just below my stinging buttocks, seeking the lips of my sex, opening me. Then a rigid cock ploughed into me; was it Jack? I wondered hazily if it was my master or not, but I didn't know or really care as I let it impale me, and then I came again, sobbing with gratitude.

Chapter Twenty-Three

'Keep still, my dear.' Lord Staith's voice was hoarse and urgent, and I felt his warm breath fan over my exposed sex. I was lying on my back, my spine rigid against the hard wooden surface of the tabletop. My legs were bent, turned outward, my knees up to my breasts, my feet jutting to the side. My hands were grasping the backs of my knees tightly, endeavouring to hold myself as still and as open as possible. My bottom was positioned right at the table's edge, so that Staith, sitting in his chair, had full access to my vulnerable sex, which was stationed mere inches from his rubicund face.

I gasped, and then held my breath, struggling not to tremble, as I felt the tip of his tongue flicker with gossamer lightness over the upper folds of my moist labia at the outer edges, just where the paleness began to darken towards the slippery brim of the divide. I frantically wondered how long I could endure this divine torture, how long I could keep still, when every fibre of my being wanted to move, to seize his silvery head and grind it convulsively into my softness. I visualised the severity of the punishment I would receive, relived the intensity of the punishment I had been given only hours before, the red weals still vividly evident on my bottom, the throbbing pain I could still feel, and held myself as still as I possibly could.

How long was it since Jane and I had been transported into our utterly servile existence? How many days had it been since we became slaves? How many weeks had passed since I have up my freedom? Three weeks? Four weeks? I had only the vaguest notion of time, which forced on me the knowledge of the shattering success of the whole operation; the endless reminders that our sole value lay in our bodies and their submission to the will of others. It was not just the punishments, though as Staith had forecast, they played a vital part in our metamorphosis. We still dreaded them, had already learnt, appallingly quickly, lots of subtle ways to reduce, at least by a fraction, their excruciating severity, by playing our slave's role to the full, by the utter passivity and acceptance of our subservience. The very way we stood, the waiting stillness that was a negation of our will, that special dumbness of our silence that totally muted our individuality and our will as individuals. It was becoming second nature to us now to behave like good little slaves. As were the cries and screams of pain, the sobbing pleas for mercy which we knew provided our masters with that extra thrill, the extra little progression towards that attainment of bliss they hungered for, their need as urgent as ours, the goal equally ephemeral, always just out of reach to possess us utterly.

But there was more to it than the physical punishment. We were never allowed to forget our bodies, or our sexual nature. We could not get away from it. After that first public chastisement all pretence of our status was cast aside. Perhaps the sickest aspect of it all was that we went along with it from the very beginning. For all my private, rebellious thoughts and my promises to myself that I would do something about it, I did absolutely nothing about it at all. I let them make a slave of me. And to my shame, deep within me was a willingness to let it happen that was more than dumb acceptance. It was like some mysteriously dark flowering inside me, taking over my rational mind, which kept protesting against my fate, a dark flower blooming deep in my soul hour by hour and day by day.

And I was forced to face the fact that its seed came from within me. It had always been there, lying unrecognised and dormant, waiting to be stimulated and watered by just the right persons and circumstances. The bizarre conditions of our capture and our victimisation by the lovely but sadistic Krista, had first caused it to awaken and grow.

Yet another powerful element in our subjection was the mirroring effect of seeing it happen to another person, the one closest to you, as I watched Jane, and she watched me, slip further and further into the helpless entrapment our minds and bodies traitorously contributed to.

Especially our bodies.

The feel of them, the caress of that balmy air on our nakedness, the insatiability of our sex drive, all these things played a part in mysteriously chaining us to our new and, as we told ourselves as a means of attempting to justify our shameful subservience, inescapable fate. We made love with each other whenever we could, which was not often, because it felt good to know that we were the same in so many ways. Then there were the five girls from the yacht, who had doubtless been given instructions to keep us simmering with need – and to satisfy that need so shatteringly that we wept with the sheer bliss of its fulfilment, no matter how many times they brought us to the dizzy heights of climax.

And there was not only lesbian loving. There was also Peter's sturdy erection, as well as increasingly casual bouts of sex with Jack. Even Carl was involved, at the command of the figures that had taken over his life as well. Preoccupied as I was with what was happening to Jane and me, I barely had time to notice that Carl seemed to be succumbing just as hopelessly to his role of slave as we were.

My thoughts spun away on an increased surge of sexual pleasure and hunger at the delicate slurping going on between my spread thighs. I was whimpering, my whole body thrumming with my efforts not to let myself slip over the rushing edge to the beautiful climax I was fast approaching. Frantically, I realised that the working mouth had withdrawn, though I could still feel the light brush of its lips, the fanning warmth of breath over my running flesh, as Staith murmured against my very cunt. I fought to concentrate on that soft, throaty whisper.

'Think of all those wonderful opportunities your lovely body possesses for one such as me, my dear.' The sticky fingers of one hand, pungent with the aroma of my sex juice, played over my features. They pressed gently on my lips and I sucked hungrily on them as they slid into my mouth, and I nibbled gently at them. They withdrew and travelled down, and briefly tweaked my nipples, which were already achingly erect.

A finger traced the narrow slit of my navel, before the

hand continued its journey downward, over my quivering belly and the damp curls of my mound, to plunge into that sweet opening awash with the fluids he had coaxed forth from me. I gasped at his fingers' possessive play over the entrance to my vagina, followed by their exquisitely slow insertion. Nothing of my most intimate flesh was spared. I winced, and flinched at last at the discomfort of a probing digit insinuating itself into the tiny fissure of my anus, groaning at the deep discomfort of its penetration, the forcing of that reluctant ring of muscle which surrendered finally, only to close again over the intruder with fierce resistance.

He held me open remorselessly, in all those sensitive areas, and I wept openly, my sprawled thighs shaking. 'Every sweet little hole in your body belongs to me, my sweet, all those divine little O's. And O is for obedience, my dear. That is all you need to remember. You understand me, yes?'

My head swam and the words echoed in my mind, as though I had heard them before, or been waiting to hear them all my life. 'Yes, my lord,' I whispered, the tears flowing freely. Already I knew when he expected, would demand, an answer from me. He pushed his mouth forward once more; his lips parted and kissed my sex in a long, lover's embrace. I shuddered, felt myself starting to come, tried to resist and lost. My tummy quivered and I flung my head back, my hair spreading wildly out across the table as I howled in ecstasy.

Days later, Jane and I were standing motionless as statues on either side of Lord Staith's chair, at the head of the long table. Perfect bondservants, we remained silent and still, moving only on command to attend on him, or Jack, or anyone else who might require our services. We no longer shared in the democratic assembly at mealtimes, had not done so since the day of our first whipping. Nor had Carl. Like us, he stood to one side, watchful and dumb. It was, as we were well aware, part of our training, to help us transform fully into our new station, as were the punishments and the increasingly casual and public use of our bodies as sex objects.

And there were other painful reminders, too. Like the small silver rings biting into our nipples. Both Jane and I had petit nipples, which meant they had to be teased and pulled and elongated to allow the spring clips to fasten into place. The vaginal rings, considerably larger, were easier to fix, nipped into the tissue of the upper folds of our labia. When we were first fitted with these adornments we both gasped, and could not hold back the tears. I did not think I would be able to endure the excruciating pain, but we were assured we would get used to it. And we did, but that fierce bite into our tender flesh was yet another constant prompting of our new servility.

'We'll have you properly pierced one of these days,' Staith promised, as though he were offering a rare treat. Mags and the others told us that the piercing, and the wearing of the rings afterwards, was less uncomfortable than the ornaments that clipped into place, but I was just as much concerned with his lordship's use of the word 'we'll'.

So, although my insides felt as though they had been sucked out of me, or as if I had stepped off the edge of a chasm into an enormous void, somewhere in the bedrock of my reeling consciousness I was not surprised when Lord Staith announced, with one of his avuncular smiles at the assembled gathering, 'I'm pleased to tell you that the girls have officially joined us. As of today, I have acquired them.' He held out his arms, beckoning us, and automatically Jane and I stepped into his embrace, felt his hands encircle our hips and pat with pride of ownership our bottoms.

'And I can tell you I've paid a far from small fortune for you,' he went on, his hands caressing our warm flesh. 'Your former master is now a man of substantial means!' He chuckled, and nodded towards Jack, at whom I was staring transfixed.

All at once I could not breathe and wondered if I was about to faint. Jack was smiling, and he met my stare without concern, but somewhere under that solid front I thought I could detect a veiled hint of some emotion, of some uncertainty – maybe even guilt. I would still like to think I did, but his face shimmered and dissolved in the tears that welled up, and I had to swallow the choking lump in my throat.

Meanwhile I heard a gasp, and then the raw and ugly sound of gut-wrenching sobs. Jane broke down completely and slumped to the ground. Her dark head fell against Staith's bare knee and her hands grasped his plump legs, her tears smeared on his tanned skin. 'No, please,' she begged. 'Please let us go. You can't...'

'But I can, my dear,' he mused. 'And I have.' His tone and air of utter confidence sent a chill up my spine. He nodded towards the athletic figure of Mags, who came forward quickly and scooped Jane up from her abject crouch, and then Staith's voice stayed at the same soothing pitch as he gave his orders, and Mags and two of her assistants swiftly carried her bodily away from the table, down towards the white sand. She was still sobbing brokenly, begging to be released, though she made no effort to resist as her cries faded.

They carried her to a simple contraption of two stout uprights joined by an overhead horizontal bar. I stood rigidly, Lord Staith's arm still resting lightly around my waist. The tears rolled silently down my face while I watched Mags and the others tie Jane's wrists over her head to the crossbar. They stood back and Mags picked up the short handled whip, and flicked it with practised skill so that the lashes fell with a sharp hiss across Jane's bottom. The livid stripes blazed over the tanned curves and she jerked, capering in a wild dance of pain.

Mags waited before she struck again, and Jane's frenzied twisting caused the weals to bite and lift across her hips and the outer sides of her thighs. Her screams rang out over the otherwise pleasantly peaceful scene, the sea rolling languidly in against the sun-drenched shore as the entranced watchers sat at the long table, enjoying an excellent buffet lunch.

The cracking strokes went on for a long time before Staith nodded, and by then Mags was glistening with perspiration. Jane hung there, slender arms stretched up to the cords that held them, her head lowered, lost in her private despair.

Staith's manicured nails ran lightly up and down the cleft of my bottom. 'While we're tying up loose ends,' he said pleasantly, 'you might like to know that your young American friend is now safe in some desert camp in South Yemen. With her blonde Germanic bitch of a mistress, of course. Oh, and by the way,' he added by way of an afterthought, smiling at Carl, 'you're mine also, of course. I have some male acquaintances who will find you absolutely enchanting, my dear fellow, as we all do.' There was a murmur of laughter from the company, both male and female.

'Yes, Lord Staith, thank you,' Carl said subserviently, standing there, slender and still pale despite the weeks of being naked beneath the tropical sun. His lowered face was carefully devoid of emotion. In the background Jane's bitter sobs died to a soft, childlike sniffling, oddly in harmony with the soothing surge of the sea.

More exciting titles available from Chimera

1-901388-65-4*	The Collector	*Steel*
1-901388-66-2*	Prisoners of Passion	*Dere*
1-901388-67-0*	Sweet Submission	*Anderssen*
1-901388-69-7*	Rachael's Training	*Ward*
1-901388-71-9*	Learning to Crawl	*Argus*
1-901388-36-0*	Out of Her Depth	*Challis*
1-901388-68-9*	Moonslave	*McLachlan*
1-901388-72-7*	Nordic Bound	*Morgan*
1-901388-27-1*	A Strict Seduction	*del Rey*
1-901388-80-8*	Cauldron of Fear	*Pope*
1-901388-74-3*	In Too Deep	*Beaufort*
1-901388-73-5*	Managing Mrs Burton	*Aspen*
1-901388-75-1*	Lucy	*Culber*
1-901388-77-8*	The Piano Teacher	*Elliot*
1-901388-25-5*	Afghan Bound	*Morgan*
1-901388-76-X*	Sinful Seduction	*Benedict*
1-901388-70-0*	Babala's Correction	*Amber*
1-901388-06-9*	Schooling Sylvia	*Beaufort*
1-901388-78-6*	Thorns	*Scott*
1-901388-79-4*	Indecent Intent	*Amber*
1-903931-00-2*	Thorsday Night	*Pita*
1-903931-01-0*	Teena Thyme	*Pope*
1-903931-02-9*	Servants of the Cane	*Ashton*
1-903931-04-5*	Captured by Charybdis	*McLachlan*
1-903931-03-7*	Forever Chained	*Beaufort*
1-903931-05-3*	In Service	*Challis*
1-903931-06-1*	Bridled Lust	*Pope*
1-903931-07-X*	Stolen Servant	*Grayson*
1-901388-21-2*	Dr Casswell's Student	*Fisher*
1-903931-08-8*	Dr Casswell's Plaything	*Fisher*
1-903931-09-6*	The Carrot and the Stick	*Vanner*
1-903931-10-X*	Westbury	*Rawlings*
1-903931-11-8*	The Devil's Surrogate	*Pope*
1-903931-12-6*	School for Nurses	*Ellis*
1-901388-30-1*	Perfect Slave	*Bell*

* * *

All **Chimera** titles are available from your local bookshop or newsagent, or direct from our mail order department. Please send your order with your credit card details, a cheque or postal order (made payable to ***Chimera Publishing Ltd***) to: **Chimera Publishing Ltd., Readers' Services, PO Box 152, Waterlooville, Hants, PO8 9FS**. Or call our **24 hour telephone/fax credit card hotline: +44 (0)23 92 783037** (Visa, Mastercard, Switch, JCB and Solo only).

To order, send: Title, author, ISBN number and price for each book ordered, your full name and address, cheque or postal order for the total amount, and include the following for postage and packing:
UK and BFPO: £1.00 for the first book, and 50p for each additional book to a maximum of £3.50.
Overseas and Eire: £2.00 for the first book, £1.00 for the second and 50p for each additional book.

*Titles £5.99. All others £4.99

For a copy of our free catalogue please write to:

Chimera Publishing Ltd
Readers' Services
PO Box 152
Waterlooville
Hants
PO8 9FS

or email us at:
sales@chimerabooks.co.uk

or purchase from our range of superb titles at:
www.chimerabooks.co.uk

Sales and Distribution in the USA and Canada

LPC Group
Client Distribution Services
193 Edwards Drive
Jackson
TN 38301
USA

Sales and Distribution in Australia

Dennis Jones & Associates Pty Ltd
19a Michellan Ct
Bayswater
Victoria
Australia 3153

* * *